Icing on the Cake

The Cupcake Club

ICing on the Cake

The Cupcake Club

Sheryl Berk and Carrie Berk

sourcebooks
jabberwocky

PJF
BERK
SHERYL

Published by Sourcebooks Jabberwocky, an imprint of Sourcebooks, Inc.
P.O. Box 4410, Naperville, Illinois 60567-4410
(630) 961-3900
Fax: (630) 961-2168
www.jabberwockykids.com

Library of Congress Cataloging-in-Publication data is on file with the publisher.

Source of Production: Versa Press, East Peoria, Illinois, USA
Date of Production: June 2013
Run Number: 20685

Printed and bound in the United States of America.
VP 10 9 8 7 6 5 4 3 2 1

To our "Maddie-cakes" for bringing puppy
love into our lives!

Photo by: Rosalie O'Connor

Mami's Secret

The aroma of her *madre's magdalenas* rising in the oven made Jenna Medina open her eyes and leap out of bed—even though it was 6 a.m. on a Sunday and the sun was barely up. The light, sweet muffins with just a hint of lemon zest were one of her favorite breakfasts and her mom's specialty, usually reserved for special occasions. It wasn't her birthday...or any of her siblings'. So why the special treat? Jenna wondered.

"Where are you going?" her big sister Gabriella grumbled. "It's too early."

"Go back to sleep," Jenna whispered. She hoped her *mami* would give her a delicate pastry right out of the oven before they were all gobbled up. That was the thing about having two older sisters and twin younger brothers—you had to fight for your share of practically everything, from food to clothes to the TV remote.

"As if I could ever sleep with all the snoring that goes on in this room!" Gabby gestured to the bunk bed above her, where Jenna's oldest sister, Marisol, was making a loud, hissing sound through her nose.

"She's worse than you are…and that's saying a lot!" Gabby groaned. She pulled the pillow over her head, trying to drown out the racket. Sharing a room with two sisters wasn't easy!

"*Buena suerte*…good luck!" Jenna chuckled. She wrapped the purple, fuzzy cupcake robe her BFF Kylie Carson had given her for Christmas over her pj's. "I'm going to see what Mami is up to."

She tiptoed down the hall of their small house and then down the stairs. She could hear her mother banging around in the cupboard. Uh-oh, Jenna suddenly thought. I hope we didn't use up all her sugar on our last cupcake order.

Peace, Love, and Cupcakes—the club and cupcake business Jenna and her four friends Kylie, Lexi, Sadie, and Delaney ran while trying to be normal fifth graders at Blakely Elementary in New Fairfield, Connecticut—had a knack for baking up a storm. Their last batch of St. Patrick's Day cupcakes had used up four dozen of her mom's eggs, Jenna recalled. Not to mention all that food coloring, flour, and vanilla extract. Kylie was sure she had bought enough to make their weekly order of two hundred cupcakes for the Golden Spoon Gourmet Grocery and four more dozen custom orders. But then Lexi decided she needed to experiment more with the color of the icing.

"I'm not sure I like the green," she sighed, piping it on a vanilla cupcake. "Does it say St. Patty's or split pea soup to you?"

Jenna shrugged. "It kinda says 'Spinach stuck in your teeth' to me. I'd put in a little more blue—but you're the artist."

Lexi closed one eye and squinted out of the other. "I say…back to the drawing board!" Jenna wasn't surprised; when it came to icing color, Lexi was very picky.

Each of the girls in the club had a special talent: Lexi, a talented artist, created beautiful fondant decorations and elegant swirls of frosting on each cupcake. Sadie, a star basketball player on the Blakely Bears team, was the most coordinated, able to crack an egg in one hand while stirring chocolate on the stove with the other. Kylie was the club's president—which meant she kept track of orders, organized meetings and baking schedules, and generally kept everything running smoothly (most of the time!). Jenna liked to think of Kylie as PLC's lemon zest—she added a "kick" to the club, whenever they needed a little push or inspiration. She reminded them what was really important ("friends and frosting!").

Delaney—who joined PLC after Kylie met her at sleep-away camp—had not only become a great baker and decorator, but also the club's DJ. She pitched in whenever PLC was overloaded with orders. Anytime the girls were stressing over a crazy deadline, Delaney would crank up her iPod and break into song and dance (usually Lady Gaga, Katy Perry, or Adele). It was so much fun and got everyone pumped up.

When Jenna complained last week that she was tired of the usual sound track and wanted some Latin rhythms, Delaney obliged. She jumped on the couch and sang "La Bamba" into a wooden spoon. Delaney was a riot—and the only person Jenna knew who could sing the entire "Gangnam Style" in the original Korean!

"How did you memorize that?" Sadie gasped. "I can barely memorize my multiplication tables!" Sadie had dyslexia and found anything involving numbers a challenge since they often appeared backward. Still, she had conquered her math phobia and become a valuable member of the PLC team—even leading the girls in a recent *Battle of the Bakers* competition on TV. They hadn't come in first place, but received a special award for being the youngest bakers in the competition—and a check that paid for an awesome new icing printer.

Delaney smiled. "I am a whiz with lyrics. Anything I need to learn, I sing. I got a 98 on my American history test because I could rap the entire Preamble!"

Then there was Jenna. Kylie made her the official taster for the cupcake club right after their first meeting. Jenna had to admit she had some talented taste buds. She could tell with one bite what type of vanilla (Madagascar? Tahitian? Mexican?) went into a cake batter or what brand of chocolate (Callebaut from Belgium? Amadei from Italy? El Rey from Venezuela?).

While other kids at Blakely Elementary teased her about being overweight, her friends never judged her. That was the thing about PLC: everyone appreciated each other for the unique talents they possessed—and the special people they were.

In a family of five kids where she landed smack in the middle, being appreciated was all Jenna ever wanted. She felt most of the time like she got lost in the crowd. She wasn't as pretty as Gabby or as smart as Marisol. And her twin brothers, Enrique and Emanuel, were just too much trouble to compete with. They were six years old and in kindergarten at Blakely. Kylie had nicknamed them "Tweedle Dee and Tweedle Dum," but Jenna preferred "the Disaster Duo." Wherever they went, chaos followed.

This morning was no different: the living room looked like a tornado had swept through it. There were toys, blocks, sneakers—even a tube of toothpaste—scattered around the room. Manny was busy building with Legos in a corner, and Ricky...where was Ricky?

"You the only one up?" Jenna asked, peering behind the sofa and in the closet. Ricky loved to jump out and scare her to death, and she suspected that was what he was plotting.

"He's with Mami mixing cake." Manny pointed to the kitchen. "He says he's going to join your cupcake club."

Jenna bristled at the thought. That's all she needed: her crazy little brother finger painting the walls of Blakely with frosting. She knew Kylie would feel the same, but Juliette, their club advisor, always reminded them, "the more the merrier." She didn't think anyone who wanted to join a club should be excluded. She'd never met Ricky.

"Cake? You mean *magdelenas*. My favorite Spanish sweet!" Jenna replied.

"No. She said it's a wedding cake."

Jenna looked puzzled. "A wedding cake? Why would Mami be making a wedding cake?"

Manny scratched his chin—that's what he did whenever he was thinking something over. "Dunno."

"*Ay, dios mío!*" Jenna exclaimed. It was her Spanish version of "OMG." She would have to get to the bottom of this.

She barged through the kitchen door and found her mother and Ricky at the counter frosting a white cake.

"*Buenos días, mija!*" Her mom smiled brightly. Ricky held up his hands, covered in frosting: "*Hola*, Jenna!"

"Everyone is up so early today," said a voice behind her. It was her mother's boyfriend, Leo. Jenna spun around and gave him an icy stare. What was *he* doing here?

He tried to kiss her on the top of her head, but Jenna pulled away. Hadn't she made it clear every time he was here that she didn't like him? Her mother had scolded her for practically ignoring him the entire Christmas Eve dinner. Jenna had kept her face buried in her plate of *cordero asado*—her mom's famous roast lamb.

"You're very quiet, Jenna," Leo had remarked. "Hope you're not feeling *baaaa-d*." Manny and Ricky cracked up and began making more barnyard animal sounds.

Jenna didn't glance up once from her plate. She didn't know what her mother saw in this guy! He thought he was funny…but he wasn't. And no one was about to out-pun her.

She picked up a plate of veggies and pushed it under his nose. "Would you like some? You know what they say at the holidays: 'Peas on Earth, goodwill toward man?'"

Leo slapped his hand on his thigh. "Now *that's* a great one!" He laughed out loud. "But I find your mother's orange flan more a-pealing. Get it? Oranges are a-pealing?" He continued to laugh 'til his cheeks turned red and his eyes watered.

Jenna glanced around the table: everyone was cracking up at his dumb joke. Everyone except her.

"He's very handsome and smart," Marisol leaned over and whispered. What did she know? She was a junior in high school and totally boy-crazy!

"And he works in manufacturing for Ralph Warren, the famous fashion designer," Gabby sighed. "Do you think he could get me that red gown Taylor Swift wore to the Grammys for my spring dance?"

Jenna's mom was just as smitten as her sisters. From the moment Leo Winters came into the dry cleaning store where she worked as a seamstress and remarked how beautiful and neat her stitches were, she was practically head over heels.

"We have so much in common," she told Jenna. "We both love fashion and the Yankees and food! Leo loves my cooking!"

Well, that was clear. He made himself a guest in their house every other Friday night for dinner—whenever it was his ex-wife's turn to take their daughter.

"He's such a devoted *papi* to his little girl," her mother cooed.

Jenna's dad was anything but devoted. He had packed his bags suddenly one day when she was only five years old and the twins were babies. She remembered that he simply kissed her on both cheeks and walked out the door. No explanation, no good-bye. Most of the other details were fuzzy: her mom crying, her sister Marisol standing at the door and waiting for him to return.

But he never did. It was like he simply vanished off the face of the Earth. She knew Marisol pretended he was in heaven—at least that's what she told her friends. But

Jenna knew the truth—he was alive and well and living in Ecuador with his new family. Her *abuela* talked about it with Jenna when she went to visit her relatives in Ecuador last summer.

"Do you want to talk to him?" her grandmother asked her one day. "I can call."

Jenna shook her head. "No. He's gone." She could never forgive him, and she didn't need him. The Medinas stood by each other and they survived. Jenna's mom got a job at Dress 4 Success Dry Cleaning, and her two sisters worked there on weekends and in the summers once they were in high school. They didn't have a lot of money or a lot of "stuff," but they had each other, and that's all they ever needed.

Until *he* came along.

"Leo's a really nice guy," Marisol told Jenna. "He makes Mami happy."

Jenna wanted to see her mother happy. But she wasn't convinced that Leo was the answer. He tried too hard—and it got on her nerves.

On her eleventh birthday in January, he showed up with an extravagant present. "I hear you're a Yankees fan like your mother," he said. He tossed her an autographed ball. "That's Derek Jeter's signature."

Jenna caught it and rolled it between her fingers. "Wonder how much I can get for this on eBay."

"Jenna!" her mother scolded her in Spanish. "*Dar las gracias!*"

But Jenna wasn't about to say "Thank you" or apologize for how she felt. Nothing he could do or say would ever change that. But Leo kept pushing.

Today, he was determined to show his expertise in the kitchen. This should be good for a laugh, Jenna smirked. He tied on one of her mother's aprons and stuck a finger in the vanilla frosting.

"Hmmm, *delicioso!*" he said, taking a lick. He then kissed her mother on the lips. Jenna wrinkled her nose and turned away.

"I see where you get your baking talent from, Jenna," he added. "You know my daughter, Maggie, is your age. I told her about your cupcake club, and she said it sounded—I quote—'awesome.' Maybe she could help you guys out sometime?"

First Ricky wanted to join PLC…now Maggie? Things were getting worse by the moment! Jenna ignored the question and sat down on a stool to watch her mother frost the cake.

"You like my cake?" her mom asked Leo.

"It's *bonita*, Betty…just like you."

If they kiss again I'm going to scream! Jenna thought.

"It's a wedding cake," Ricky piped up.

"No, not a wedding cake. An engagement cake," her mother corrected him.

"Why are you baking an engagement cake? Who's engaged?" Jenna asked.

Her mother smiled and held out her hand. On it was a sparkly pear-shaped diamond ring. "I am!"

Jenna stared at the ring…then at her mother…then at the ring again.

This wasn't happening. It couldn't be! She didn't want a stepfather or a stepsister. She didn't want a wedding or an engagement or anything in their lives to change. She liked things the way they were, even if they were crowded and a little chaotic.

Just then, Gabby and Marisol came bounding into the kitchen in their pj's. "Manny told us…let me see the ring!" Gabby gushed, grabbing her mother's hand. "OMG, it's gorgeous!"

"And huge!" Marisol added. She turned to Leo. "Tell me all the deets—how did you pop the question? Did you surprise her?"

Leo blushed. "It was nothing…"

"Oh, yes it was!" Jenna's mother insisted. "It was the

most romantic night of my entire life!" She kissed Leo and Jenna's sisters cheered: "*Beso! Beso!* Kiss! Kiss!" Her mother obliged, flinging her arms around Leo's neck.

Jenna rolled her eyes. Her *madre* was behaving like a lovesick teenager. In fact, she was worse. Marisol's idea of romance with her boyfriend, Wyatt, was a Knicks game on TV and a frozen pizza in the oven. Couldn't her mom be content with that? Why did she have to go and ruin everything and get married?

"How did you propose?" Marisol pumped Leo for information. "Did you get down on one knee?"

Leo nodded. "I did. I said, '*¿Quieres casarte conmigo?*' and my beautiful Betty said yes."

Jenna winced. She hated when Leo spoke in Spanish. He usually confused the tenses or pronounced things wrong. Just because he worked for Ralph Warren's international sales division did not make him an expert on languages—though he liked to brag that he spoke Spanish, French, Italian, Mandarin, and Japanese fluently.

Everything about Leo irritated her. His ties were hideous (his favorite was blue with red ladybugs on it), and he wore polka-dot socks with his business suits. He thought he was a gourmet chef but had burned the lasagna last Friday. And then there was his taste in music.

Jenna would never forget how Leo's attempt at a gourmet dinner had nearly set their kitchen on fire.

"*O sole mio!*" his voice had boomed as he sprinkled shredded mozzarella on a pile of noodles for the lasagna.

"You sing good," Ricky remarked, scooping a handful of cheese out of the bowl.

"You sing *well*," Jenna corrected him.

"Why, thank you for the compliment!" Leo winked at her. "I'm no CeeLo, but I try."

Jenna groaned and gritted her teeth as he continued to serenade her while preparing dinner. He popped it in the oven, forgetting to set the timer for fifty minutes.

"I think your mother will be surprised that I decided to cook, don't you?" he asked her.

Jenna shrugged. "I guess."

"She works very hard. I'd like to make her life easier and happier. I don't know anyone who deserves it more."

☆ ☮ ☆

Now that she thought about it, Leo hadn't just been talking about lasagna last Friday. He was hinting that he wanted to marry her mother. Why hadn't she realized it a week ago? Maybe she could have stopped him. Maybe she could have talked her *mami* out of it.

She wished her sisters were on her side—but they seemed just as smitten with Leo as her mom was.

"Did he surprise you? Did he hide the ring?" Marisol demanded.

Her mother beamed. "Oh, it was so *romántico*: wine, candlelight, my favorite Portuguese tapas restaurant in New York City…" She and Leo locked lips yet again.

"Ugh! Spare me!" Jenna grumbled. She'd had enough. "I'm starving! Can we *please* eat breakfast?"

Her mother looked hurt. "*Mija*, aren't you happy for us? I thought you'd love to be a bridesmaid."

Jenna shook her head. "Bridesmaid dresses are ugly."

"Not when your mother makes them," Leo insisted. "What color dresses will you make, *mi amor*?"

Gabby's hand shot up. "Ooh! How about emerald green? That's my color. It looks great with my auburn hair. Strapless with a short, puffy skirt."

"No, no…white…with a long, mermaid skirt," Marisol corrected her.

"Actually, I was thinking metallic gold," Jenna's mom insisted. "*Perfecto* for a Las Vegas wedding, don't you think?'

"Vegas!" Gabby and Marisol started jumping up and down.

"What's Vegas?" Ricky asked.

"It's tacky…" Jenna protested. "And loud and crazy."

Ricky and Manny both liked the sound of that. "Vegas! Vegas!" they chanted.

"It's a place in Nevada where we can have a huge fiesta and invite all our family and friends," Leo explained. "I have a sales conference at a hotel there in a month, and we thought it would be the perfect place to tie the knot."

"*Sí*, on your spring break from school. We'll all fly out and have the wedding and a vacation," Jenna's mother added.

Spring break? Her mother was planning on getting married in four weeks? Jenna's head was spinning! She had to do something!

"I can't…we can't," she stammered. "Easter is one of our busiest seasons for Peace, Love, and Cupcakes. We already have orders for dozens of 'Somebunny Loves Me' carrot cupcakes and I *cannot* cancel!"

"Can't your friends carry on without you?" Leo suggested.

"Carry on? Without me?" Jenna gasped. Clearly Leo

had no idea how important a role she played in the cupcake club's business.

"Since this is such a special occasion, I'm sure they wouldn't mind," he said.

"But I do!" Jenna shouted.

"I do! I do!" Gabby teased her. "That's what Mami is going to say!"

Jenna was never one to let her emotions show—she was able to keep a stone face even when bullies at school called her "fatty" or "bubble butt" or "thunder thighs." But this was too much to take. She felt like everyone was ganging up on her, ignoring her opinion. When it came to cupcakes, her thumbs-up or thumbs-down on the flavor of batter or frosting was always the final word. When Kylie suggested a peppermint-stick cupcake for Christmas and Jenna vetoed it ("The icing tastes like toothpaste!"), her friends respected her decision. But no one in her house cared what she thought or felt.

"I don't want a stupid wedding!" Jenna blurted out. Then she glared at Leo. "And I don't want a new *papi*!"

☆ ☮ ☆

Kylie Carson had never heard her friend so upset. She tried

to calm her down on the phone, but thought it was best to let Jenna get things off her chest.

"Can you believe it? They're getting married, and they didn't even ask what I thought! How could my *madre* do this to me?"

"I don't think she did it to *you*," Kylie tried to reassure her. "I think she's in love. Which is kind of nice...don't you think?"

"It's gross," Jenna protested. "You should see how mushy they are around each other..."

"When's the wedding?" Kylie asked.

"It's completely ridiculous! They want to get married in a month in Vegas, right in the middle of Easter. What about all our orders? How inconsiderate is that?"

"It'll be tough, but we'll be okay," Kylie reassured her. "We'll just have to start planning a lot earlier than we thought, maybe freeze some of the cupcakes, and finish them up without you."

"No way!" Jenna interrupted her. She knew Kylie was trying to be practical, but this was not what she needed to hear. "You are not doing all those Easter orders without me!"

"Jenna, it's your mom's wedding. You need to be there," Kylie said gently.

"Says who?" Jenna shot back. "I can stay over at your house. I hate Leo, and I don't want to see my mother ruin her life by marrying him!"

Just then, she noticed her mother standing in the doorway of her bedroom. There were tears in her eyes.

"Mami," she said softly. "I'm sorry."

Her mother shook her head. "I thought you'd be happy. A real family, Jenna. A *papi* who cares about you and loves you."

Jenna didn't know what to say. She knew her mother's feelings were hurt, but she was hurt too.

"I was coming up to ask if you and the girls would make a cupcake wedding cake," her mother said.

"Yes! Yes!" Jenna heard Kylie yelling on the other end of the phone.

"I don't know," Jenna replied. "We're very busy."

"We'll do it!" Kylie continued to shout. "Jenna, it'll be amazing!"

"I'll think about it," Jenna said, hiding the receiver under her pillow so her mother couldn't hear Kylie pleading.

Her mom's face lit up. "*Sí?* Leo will be so happy! I am so happy!" She handed Jenna a recipe for *tres leches* cake. "*Mi favorita*," she said. "Your grandma's secret recipe." She hugged Jenna tight.

"I didn't say yes," Jenna tried to explain. "I said maybe." But her mom was already out the door. She spoke English fluently, but sometimes—when she didn't want to hear the word *no*—she pretended not to.

"Hello? Hello?" Jenna heard a muffled voice from under her pillow. She'd almost forgotten about Kylie!

"I'm here," Jenna replied. "She wants us to make *tres leches* cupcakes."

"Awesome!" Kylie said, getting down to business. "We'll meet tomorrow after school, and Lexi can sketch out a design for the tower."

"I don't know who's worse: you or my mom." Jenna sighed. "We can't ship a huge cupcake tower to Las Vegas, which means we'll have to bake and assemble it there."

"Jenna, this is amazing!" Kylie squealed. "I can't wait to tell the girls."

3

"Bean" There, Done That

Every meeting of the cupcake club began the same way. Juliette Dubois, the club's advisor, tapped her wooden spoon on the countertop of the teachers' lounge kitchen at Blakely Elementary. "Settle down, ladies! I call this meeting of Peace, Love, and Cupcakes to order!" Once they were all quiet, she handed the spoon to Kylie who carefully went over old and new business. Since Kylie was the first to join the club—and recruit the others—she was the one who led it.

"Okay, let's start with accounting." Kylie flipped to the chart in her notebook that kept track of how much they were making versus how much they were spending. "Lexi, we spent $150 on shredded coconut this month?"

"I'm stocking up for Easter," Lexi explained. "Coconut makes adorable bunny fur on cupcakes." Lexi was always thinking of ways to "push the envelope" on their cupcake decorations. She thought cupcakes were not just delicious treats; they were works of art.

"And, Jenna, you ordered $100 worth of jelly beans?" Kylie continued. She pointed to several jars of rainbow-colored candies on the shelf that Jenna had labeled according to brand and flavor. Jenna would never settle for merely an ordinary bean or a humdrum hunk of chocolate. Every ingredient had to taste the very best—her sophisticated palate demanded it and PLC's clients demanded it.

"I wasn't sure which ones were the yummiest: Jelly Belly, Teenee Beanee, or Starburst," she explained. "It was a close one."

"Do we get to do a taste test too? I love jelly beans!" Sadie piped up.

Jenna got a mischievous look in her eye. "Sure!" she said. "See for yourself. These are my faves."

She got a few out of the jars and handed a blue jelly bean to Sadie, an orange and brown one to Lexi, a green one to Delaney, and a dark brown one to Kylie.

"Close your eyes and guess the flavor," she instructed them.

Sadie popped the candy in her mouth and made a face. "Eww. This is really minty. Like toothpaste!"

"Ding! Ding! Ding!" Jenna said, laughing. "That's

exactly it! It's toothpaste flavor. Don't you feel like you're brushing your teeth?"

"Mine tastes kind of plain," Delaney said, taking a nibble. "Is it earwax? Someone played a joke on me in camp and gave me that one."

"Close," Jenna replied. "It's booger flavor."

"Eww!" Delaney screamed, spitting it out. "That's disgusting!"

"You're next, Lex," Jenna said, taunting her friend to take a taste.

Lexi looked at her orangey bean from every angle. "What is it supposed to taste like? Red pepper? Salsa? I know this is going to be gross…"

"We all bit…your turn!" Sadie egged her on.

Lexi took a teeny, tiny bite and made a face. "It tastes like dirt."

"Earthworm to be exact." Jenna giggled as Lexi wiped her lips on a paper towel.

"Now you, Kylie. I saved the best for last!"

"It looks like milk chocolate," Kylie said, examining the candy.

"Oh, no. Do they make a poop flavor?" Sadie whispered to Delaney.

"Not that I've heard of," Delaney replied. "Vomit, rotten egg, and sardine, but no poop."

Kylie bravely tossed the bean in her mouth and swallowed it whole.

"Well?" Sadie asked. "What did it taste like?"

"Not that bad. Kind of savory."

"Care to take a guess on what you just gulped down?" Jenna teased.

"Well, it's not chocolate pudding. Is it cola? Cardboard? Pencil shavings?"

Jenna shook her head. "Not even close! You're *barking* up the wrong tree…"

Kylie got the hint: "Oh, no! Is it dog food?"

"Yay, Kylie's top dog!" Jenna cracked up. "I had to have some fun with you."

Kylie took a big gulp of water to wash the taste out of her mouth. "I hope the jelly beans you got for our Easter cupcakes taste better than those," she said. "Please tell me you got normal flavors."

"Relax," Jenna said. "I got the best ones ever: juicy pear, red apple, tutti-frutti, caramel corn, and toasted marshmallow."

"Great. Then we will have plenty to decorate our 'egg-citing' cupcakes with." Kylie made a check in her notebook.

"Lex, you'll pipe green grass frosting and we'll put the jelly beans on top."

Lexi nodded. "I thought I could also use them for our bunny cupcakes—the pink bubble gum ones would make a great nose and the blue ones would be perfect for eyes. As long as they're blueberry and not dead fish flavor?"

Jenna crossed her heart and raised her hand. "I promise every bean on our cupcakes will be *delicioso*." She popped a bright green one in her mouth. "But you guys really should try these spinach ones…they're tasty!"

Kylie put down her notebook. "As long as we're all set for our Easter orders, that brings us to new business. Jenna, would you like to fill the club in on our special order for your mom?"

"Your mom wants us to bake her cupcakes? What for?" Delaney asked. "Is it her birthday?" Delaney was always up for a party!

Jenna pouted. "No, I wish it were that easy." She handed out copies of her grandma's *tres leches* recipe. "My mom wants us to make these for her wedding."

"Her wedding? How? When?" Sadie asked excitedly. "That's great news!" She noticed Jenna's frown. "Isn't it?"

"The most important question is *where*," Kylie

pointed out. "Jenna's mom is getting married in a month…in Las Vegas!"

"Oh, cool!" Lexi exclaimed. "I saw this episode of *Cake Boss* once where he made a giant slot machine out of cake. How cool would it be to have a slot machine that spits our cupcakes out when you win?"

"Maybe they could have different coins made of gold and silver fondant on top?" Delaney suggested.

Jenna looked annoyed. "I'm glad you guys all think this is fun. I'm freaking out! My whole life is crazy!"

"It sounds crazy wonderful," Sadie pointed out. "We all met Leo when he picked you up at Kylie's house a few weeks ago, and he seems like a great guy."

Jenna sighed. "Not you too? Everyone loves Leo. Leo this, Leo that. I hate him!"

"Maybe you should save the booger beans for him then?" Delaney suggested. "Just sayin'…"

"But you're doing this for your mom," Juliette pointed out. "Focus on that. This will make her very happy on her big day."

"Don't leave out the best part!" Kylie elbowed Jenna. "Leo said if your parents are cool with it, he will fly us all out to Vegas to assemble the wedding cupcake display *and* to be junior bridesmaids in the wedding."

"That is phenom!" Delaney started jumping up and down. "I want to count all the neon lights on the Vegas strip!"

Kylie laughed. "Before you do that, do you think you can count how many cupcakes we'll need to build a giant six-tier wedding cake?"

Lexi was already sketching with her colored pencils. "I'm thinking four dozen on the bottom tier, three dozen on the next two tiers, two dozen on the two tiers above that, and a giant cupcake with their monogram on the top tier."

Delaney did some quick math in her head: "That's 168 cupcakes plus the giant cupcake that can serve at least twenty. Totally doable!"

Lexi held up a sketch of a giant cupcake piped with white swirled lines, white carnations, and a gold BWL monogram in gold fondant on top. "What do you think?"

"What's the W for?" Delaney asked.

"Leo's last name," Sadie explained. "Winters. Hey, Jenna Winters has a nice ring to it!"

Jenna shuddered. "Winters? Yuck! I hate winter. I hate the cold."

"How about Summers, then?" Delaney teased. "That would be hot!"

Jenna was not amused. "I'm always going to be Jenna Medina."

Juliette placed a hand on her shoulder. "I know this is hard for you," she said. "Change is never easy."

Kylie nodded. "I totally get it, Jenna," she said. "You like things the way they are. I felt that way too." She reminded her how her family had to leave Jupiter, Florida, just two years ago when her dad's company relocated them to Connecticut. "But if I hadn't come to New Fairfield, I wouldn't have met you."

"That's different," Jenna insisted. "You didn't have Leo the Loser trying to elbow into your life and ruin everything!"

"Hmmm, I thought you were tougher than that, Jenna." Juliette raised an eyebrow. "You usually don't let anyone rattle you."

That might have been the case in the school yard or the classroom when dealing with bullies, but not in her own backyard. She felt like she was being attacked by alien invaders and there was nothing she could do about it!

"If you don't want to take this order, we'll pass," Kylie said, sensing her BFF was very stressed out. "Vegas would be awesome, but you're more important."

"Please, Jenna?" Delaney pleaded. "Pretty please with frosting on top? I've always wanted to be a junior bridesmaid."

Jenna rolled her eyes. "Fine. I'll bake the cupcakes, but I'm not happy about it."

"I knew you wouldn't let us down," Kylie said, hugging her. "Or your mom."

"Yay!" Delaney, Sadie, and Lexi cheered. "We're going to Vegas!"

4

A New Leash on Life

Jenna's little brother Ricky had a talent for throwing tantrums just when she was running late to school. Her mom always had to be at her dry-cleaning store by 7 a.m., and Marisol and Gabby drove to high school together. Which left Jenna in charge of her loco little brothers and getting them all out the door for the elementary school bus pickup.

"You need to put your sneakers on!" she said, chasing Ricky around the living room.

"I don't wanna wear shoes," he cried, as Jenna tried to wrestle his purple high-tops onto his feet. "Ricky, *venga ya!*" she shouted. "Give me a break!"

Jenna did her best to double-knot the laces so they stayed put. "Can we please go to school now?" She sighed. "The bus will leave without us!" Ms. Heller had mentioned she was handing out assignments for their community friends project this morning, and Jenna wanted to get a good one.

"I don't wanna go to school," Ricky said, kicking his feet. "It's not fun."

"Kindergarten is tons of fun." Jenna tried her best to convince him. "There are ABCs and 123s…and Legos to play with."

Manny nodded. "I like Legos." She noticed he was eating Cheerios out of the box and leaving a trail of them on the living room rug. He was messy—but at least he was on time.

She turned her attention back to Ricky who was sitting cross-legged on the floor, refusing to budge. "I heard your kindergarten teacher say she was going to read you a really cool story today about the Easter Bunny," Jenna said, trying to bait him. "Hippity, hoppity!"

Ricky looked up. "Yeah? What's his name?"

Jenna knew it was Peter Cottontail, but thought that would never entice Ricky enough to walk to the end of the block and get on the Blakely school bus.

"Um, his name is José Starfighter—and he brings water balloons and video games to good little boys who go to school on time!" she improvised.

"Cool!" Ricky laughed. "I wanna meet him!"

Jenna handed him his lunch box and smiled. "Then *vámonos!*"

☆ ☮ ☆

Once she had deposited the Disaster Duo in their kindergarten classrooms, Jenna raced to her social studies class on the third floor. She slid into her chair and quickly unpacked, just as her teacher unveiled a large poster on the wall.

"This is the Wheel of Caring," Ms. Heller explained. "Everyone will get a chance to spin. Whatever you land on will be the organization you will learn about."

Meredith Mitchell's hand shot up. "Me, me, me!" She waved at Ms. Heller.

"Fine, Meredith, you're up." She flicked the spinner and watched as it landed on Shop for a Cause.

"Woo-hoo!" she cheered. "I get to shop! I am *so* good at that!"

Great, Jenna groaned. It was just like Meredith to land the easiest assignment!

"Not exactly," Ms. Heller explained. "Shop for a Cause is an Internet agency that arranges items to be donated. Then people go online and purchase them, and the money goes to various charities."

"So I don't get to buy *anything*?" Meredith whined. "That is so not fair!" She stomped back to her seat.

"Jenna, you're next." Her teacher spied her smirking at her desk in the back of the room. "Let's have a good one!"

Jenna looked over the wheel—there were lots of great options. Baking for Good sounded right up her alley, and so did the Hispanic Heritage Society. She could even get into researching the Believe Charity Drive, since she knew it was Justin Bieber's cause. She closed her eyes, crossed her fingers, and spun the wheel as hard as she could. It landed on Rescue Rover.

"Great!" Ms. Heller clapped her hands. "You got the new dog rescue shelter opening in Danbury."

"Um, I don't really know much about dogs," Jenna said. "Maybe you wanna give this one to someone who does?"

Again, Meredith's hand shot up. "Ooh, ooh! Ms. Heller, I'll trade. I have a teacup poodle named Fifi Le Cute at home!"

"Of course you do," Jenna muttered under her breath. Was there anything Meredith didn't have?

"Sorry, you get what you get…and for Jenna, that's pets!" Ms. Heller sang. She handed Jenna a brochure with a fluffy white puppy on the cover. "Try and set up a time to visit after school," she told Jenna. "And take lots of notes."

36

Jenna wasn't sure what she could do for a bunch of dogs that needed homes. Her house was crowded enough—and her sisters barked at each other already. She phoned the Canine Help Line and asked to speak to the person in charge.

"That would be me!" said a perky voice on the other end. "I'm Lucky."

Jenna chuckled. Was that a person's name...or a cocker spaniel's?

"Oh, hi…I'm Jenna Medina. I'm in the fifth grade at Blakely Elementary School, and I'd like to interview you for my community studies project." Jenna opened her notebook. "Can I ask you a few questions?"

"Nope," Lucky replied. "You need to come to our shelter and see for yourself!" She dictated the address and dismissed Jenna with "See ya soon!"

Her mom and her sisters were both at work, which left one person at home with a car—the last person she wanted to ask for help.

"*Qué pasa*, Jenna?" Leo smiled. He was working on his laptop on the couch, going through projected sales figures for the new Ralph Warren resort collection. Great, Jenna thought, he's already made himself at home!

"I need to do some research in Danbury," she said. "I don't suppose you have time to take me?"

"I'd love to!" Leo leaped to his feet. "Let me get my keys, and we'll be on our way in a jiffy!"

Jenna didn't know what a "jiffy" was, nor did she care. She just needed to get her homework done. She barely said a word on the ride over—not even when Leo pressed her for more details on her assignment.

"So where do the dogs come from? How many of them are placed in homes? Do you like dogs? What kind are your favorites?" He fired questions at her.

"I dunno," was all she replied. "Are we there yet?"

Rescue Rover was located in a small, white storefront with large glass windows out front. In them were adorable dogs playing and pouncing on each other.

"Aww, look at that little guy!" Leo said, pointing to a dachshund chasing his tail.

But Jenna's gaze zoned in on a tiny, black-and-white fluff ball hanging out in a corner. The dog was busily chomping on a chew toy, but when Jenna tapped her fingers on the window, the puppy sprang forward to try and greet her.

"That's our little eight-week-old Havanese," said a

woman's voice. Jenna suspected it was Lucky. "You wanna see her?"

"Actually, I'm Jenna. I'm here to interview you. We talked on the phone?" Jenna noticed that the puppy was still leaping against the window, trying to get her attention.

"Of course! Come on in!" The woman pushed the door open. "But I think the best way to understand our organization is to talk to some of our rescues."

Jenna looked around. Clearly, Lucky was loco. There was no one else in the shelter except a dozen or so dogs.

"You want me to interview the dogs?" she asked. "Um, I speak English and Spanish…not puppy."

Lucky lifted the Havanese out of the window and placed it on Jenna's lap. "That's okay. Just listen…"

The little dog snuggled against Jenna and licked her fingers. Then she gazed up and gave a tiny *yap*!

"Aww, she wants you to pick her up," Leo cooed.

Jenna wanted to ask, "Really? You speak dog *and* Spanish?" but held her tongue. Instead, she lifted the little bundle in her arms and cradled her. She would never admit it to Leo or Lucky, but this dog was pretty darn adorable!

"What is she telling you?" Lucky asked.

"Um, 'Bowwow, how are ya?'" Jenna guessed.

"She's telling you she wants to be loved and she needs a good home," Lucky replied.

Jenna looked into the puppy's dark blue eyes and her heart melted. "Me? She wants me?"

"Can't you tell?" Lucky smiled. "She's saying it loud and clear!"

"Where did she come from?" asked Leo.

"Where most of the dogs here at Rescue Rover come from." Lucky sighed. "She was abandoned on the side of a road by her owners. Someone found the litter of puppies and called us, and we brought them here."

"That's so sad," Jenna said, scratching the puppy under her chin. "She's so tiny and helpless."

"Our job is to rescue, rehabilitate, and place homeless dogs with loving new families," Lucky explained. "We're just getting off the ground. This weekend is our grand opening party."

A lightbulb went off over Jenna's head. "I want to help," she said. "I have a cupcake club, and we could bake cupcakes for your party."

"That would be wonderful!" Lucky exclaimed. The little puppy barked her approval as well.

"Does she have a name?" Jenna asked. "What do you call her?"

"Well, she was found on the highway right by the Brewster exit—so we call her Brewster," Lucky explained.

Jenna made a face. "Oh, no! This is not a Brewster!" She lifted the puppy up to her face until they were nose to nose. "You're too sweet to be a Brewster. That's it! I'll call you Dulce—that means sweet in Spanish!"

The puppy gave Jenna a lick as if to say, "I like it!"

"So Dulce and I will expect you on Saturday at ten a.m.," Lucky said. "Tell everyone to come!"

As they left the animal shelter, Jenna couldn't help but notice a strange feeling in the pit of her stomach. It wasn't the hunger pains that usually rumbled her tummy. It was more a sensation of sad emptiness.

"I hate to leave Dulce there," she said, watching out of the car window as Leo slowly pulled out of the Rescue Rover parking lot. "I miss her already."

"Sounds like that pup made a pretty strong impression on you," he commented.

"She did. I just can't bear to think of her all alone in the world!"

Leo nodded. "I understand how you feel, Jenna, but someone will adopt her soon. You'll see."

☆ ☮ ☆

That night at dinner, Jenna barely touched her *arroz con pollo*. All she could think about was the tiny puppy that had snuggled in her arms.

"Couldn't we adopt her, Mami?" she blurted out. "I'd take care of her and walk her. I'm really responsible. If I can handle Ricky and Manny, I can handle a dog!"

"*Sí*, I know you are," Jenna's mother replied. "But the house is so crowded already. Where would we put a dog?"

"In my room," Jenna volunteered.

"You mean our room," Marisol corrected her. "And no way. I trip over all your junk on the floor already."

"Then I suppose I have some good news," Leo said, wiping his mouth with a napkin. "Your mother and I saw a 'For Sale' sign on a bigger house just a few blocks away. It needs a little fixing up, but we thought it would be perfect for our new *familia*. I made the owners an offer...and they accepted."

Jenna's mom threw her arms around Leo's neck and hugged him. "*Qué sorpresa maravillosa!* What a wonderful surprise!"

"A new house?" Gabby exclaimed. "Awesome! Do I get my own room?"

"Marisol is the oldest, so we thought she should get her own room, which will be yours when she goes to college in a few years," Leo said.

"Yes!" Marisol pumped her fist in the air. "No more sisters snoring!"

"You and Jenna will share, and Ricky and Manny will have their own room," he added. "And there will be an extra room for Maggie when she stays over."

"Maggie?" Jenna gasped. "She's coming to live with us, but we can't get a little puppy?"

"Um, she's Leo's daughter," Gabby whispered. "Not a pet. And FYI, I am painting our room neon green—like it or not."

☆ ☮ ☆

"Neon green? She really said neon green?" Kylie asked Jenna as they packed up the weekly cupcake order for Mr. Ludwig at the Golden Spoon. The club was hard at work in Kylie's kitchen, whipping up six dozen strawberry champagne cupcakes and six dozen salted caramel cupcakes for the gourmet shop.

Jenna stirred the sugar in a small pot with butter and cream until it melted and browned. "Gooey-licious," she said, taking a whiff. "Caramel's ready."

"It could be worse," Delaney pointed out. "She could have said she wanted to paint your room neon yellow. Or black with red polka dots."

"That's not the worst part," Jenna explained, taking the pot off the stove so it could cool. "Leo's kid is moving in too. He gets her every other week, and she's my age and gets her own room!" She swiped her finger along the edge of one of the cupcakes and tasted the frosting.

"It's so not fair!" she said with her mouth full, taking another big lick.

"Hey! No eating the order! I don't have any extra frosting," Lexi said, snatching the cupcake out of Jenna's hands.

"Sorry, Lex," Jenna moped. "When I'm stressed, I eat."

"Is it really so bad?" Sadie asked. "I mean, a new house sounds pretty cool."

"It's not the house, it's who's in it," Jenna replied. "Leo."

"I thought you said he drove you to the dog shelter so you could do your community friends project," Delaney reminded her. "That was nice of him."

"And those photos you posted of that puppy on Instagram were adorable," Sadie pointed out. "What did you say her name was?"

"*Dul-say*," Jenna pronounced it for them. "Oh, and I also promised Rescue Rover we'd make cupcakes for their grand opening this weekend."

"What?" Kylie gasped. "How many?" She flipped through their order book. "We're maxed out this weekend!"

"Oops, I guess I got so upset over the whole house thing that I forgot to put it in the order book and tell you guys."

Kylie shook her head. "Jenna, you can't make promises without checking with us."

"I know! I know!" Jenna cried. "But this is a canine cupcake emergency!"

"How many?" Lexi said, piping a red rose on a cupcake for an anniversary order. "Are we talking a dozen...or twelve dozen?"

"Well, they do expect a big crowd," Jenna said softly. "And then there are the cupcakes that the dogs can eat..."

"Whoa! You need cupcakes for dogs too?" Kylie said. "That's a lot of work in just three days."

"But doable!" Jenna tried to convince her. "We've had crazier deadlines before." She took out her phone and held up a photo she had snapped of Dulce. "Can you honestly say no to this sweet face?"

"I'm the one who has to decorate them. Do I get a say?" Lexi asked. She wiped a dot of sweat off her brow and left a streak of red frosting in its place.

Jenna pouted and made puppy-dog eyes at Lexi. "Woof, woof!" she barked. "Come on, Lex!"

"Fine…just don't lick me!" Lexi giggled. "Down, girl, down!" She patted Jenna on the head.

Sadie took a pen and paper and started making a list. "We'll need bananas, whole wheat flour, honey—what else do dogs like?"

"Peanut butter," Lexi said. "My dog is nuts about peanut butter."

Sadie added "PB" to their grocery list. "Anything else?"

"Better put down six dozen more eggs and another bottle of vanilla," Jenna pointed out. "Just to be sure."

"I think we should do minis for the dogs and full-size for the people," Kylie said. "Maybe build a bone sculpture out of cupcakes?" She printed out several photos of dog breeds off her laptop and handed them to Lexi. "Think you can make these out of fondant?" she asked.

Lexi nodded. "Totally. Delaney can do the bodies and I'll do the faces. Sadie, can you do some dog bones and bowls out of fondant?"

"Aye-aye!" Sadie saluted.

"You see, there's nothing PLC can't do with a little teamwork." Jenna smiled. It was the happiest she'd felt since the dreadful news of her mom's engagement. Maybe Ms. Heller was right; giving back to the community really did make you feel great.

In fact, she felt a pun coming on…

"I hate to *hound* you with a last-minute order," she joked. "But I know nothing is too *ruff* for PLC to handle."

5

A Fido Fiesta

First thing Saturday morning, Kylie and Jenna loaded large boxes filled with cupcakes and pupcakes into the trunk and the back of Leo's car to deliver to the dog shelter. The other girls agreed they would make the rest of the deliveries for the day with Sadie's brothers. When they pulled up to Rescue Rover, Lucky and Dulce greeted them at the door.

"*Hola, perrita!*" Jenna said as the little dog danced around her ankles. "Meet my friend Kylie."

"Aw, she's so cute!" Kylie exclaimed. "I hope you like pupcakes, puppy."

"All our guests do," Lucky said, motioning to a pack of dogs running around a giant exercise pen. "That's Frito, that's Lulu, that's Milkbone, that's Curly, that's Romeo... and that huge Great Dane there is Trixie."

"And this is Dulce," Jenna said, kneeling down. "Isn't she delicious?"

Once in her arms, the tiny dog settled her head on Jenna's shoulder, hiding beneath her dark brown hair and nuzzling her neck.

"She really loves you, Jenna," Kylie said.

"What's not to love?" Jenna joked. "Besides, I put a dab of vanilla behind each ear as perfume."

Kylie rolled her eyes. "I never know when you're joking or being serious!"

"That makes two of us," Leo chimed in. "Maybe you can help me decipher the mysterious Miss Medina?"

Kylie laughed. "Sounds like a case for Scotland Yard…"

Great, thought Jenna, just what I need. Leo cozying up to my best friend to brainwash her too!

"Do you like Sherlock Holmes mysteries?" Leo asked.

"Are you kidding? *The House of Fear* is one of my faves!"

"But what about *Sherlock Holmes and the Voice of Terror*?" Leo asked.

"Classic!" Kylie exclaimed.

Enough was enough. The last thing Jenna needed was for Kylie to start comparing old scary movies with Leo! "No time for small talk," she said, tugging Kylie by the arm and Dulce by her leash. "Gotta go set up for the fido fiesta!"

They unpacked the boxes of mini pupcakes and began

sticking them with peanut butter to a giant Styrofoam bone that Lexi had sculpted. "*Perfecto!*" Jenna remarked. "Maybe PLC should consider adding more 'pawstries' to our menu."

Kylie laughed. "I can see it now: 'Make no bones about it: PLC's gone to the dogs!' Honestly, I think dogs would be easier to please than some of our clients."

She opened a box and checked that all the intricate fondant dog toppers on the cupcakes were in good shape. "So far, no crushed cocker spaniels or ruined Rottweilers…"

"And the terriers look terrific!" Jenna chimed in.

Kylie delicately placed a few cupcakes on a silver platter. "Do you think our doggies need doilies? Or is that too fancy?"

"I think we should put them on white paper napkins to look like wee-wee pads," Jenna chuckled.

"That would be really funny!" Kylie agreed. "I think I saw some with the sandwiches out front." She went to search, leaving Jenna with Dulce and her puppy playmates.

"Your family is bigger than mine," Jenna observed, watching Dulce run with the pack in circles. She noticed that Dulce often got edged out of the group and left behind—the same way Jenna did in the Medina clan. Her mother was with Leo; Ricky and Manny were a duo; Gabby and Marisol stuck together like glue. That always left her out in the cold. Just like Dulce, she was always fighting to maintain her place in the circle.

She stepped in and scooped up the little puppy before she could get trampled again. "I know how you feel, girl," she said, stroking Dulce's furry head. "Nobody pays much attention to you. But I will. I even brought you a present." She sat down on the floor and pulled a chew toy out of her pocket. It was shaped like a cupcake. She tossed it high in the air and called, "Fetch!" Dulce scampered after it.

Just then, she heard a loud noise and lots of excited barks behind her. The entire display of pupcakes went crashing to the floor as Trixie pounced on it.

"Wait! No!" Jenna screamed. But it was too late; the dogs were devouring the pupcakes, and it was all she could do to wrestle the Styrofoam bone away before that was in shreds. Kylie, Leo, and Lucky came running.

"Oh, no! The pupcakes!" Kylie cried.

"Looks like Miss Trixie is up to her old tricks," Lucky said. "She's a master at getting the latch on the pen gate open. I guess she smelled your treats and couldn't wait to have a taste."

Jenna stared in disbelief: all that was left of their pup-cake sculpture was a pile of crumbs. Dulce hopped into the center of the mob and nabbed a few.

"All our hard work," Jenna sighed. "Gobbled up before anyone got to see it."

"Doggone dogs," Leo said, trying to brighten the mood. "Where are their manners? Don't they know you wait to eat until all the guests have arrived?"

"Well, at least we have plenty of beautiful cupcakes left for the people coming," Lucky said. "Save me a vanilla Maltese one—I'm going to open the doors. It's noon!"

The afternoon flew by with lots of praise for PLC's cupcakes and lots of adoptions for the dogs at Rescue Rover. Jenna wanted Dulce to find a good, loving family, but she secretly hoped no one would take her away. By 4 p.m., most of the crowd had cleared out, and the tiny Havanese puppy remained in her crate. Jenna heaved a sigh of relief.

"I guess we're meant to be together for a little longer," she said, reaching in to tickle the puppy's tummy. "I'll come back and visit you in a few days, I promise."

☆ ☮ ☆

Jenna's report was due Monday morning, and she decided, as Lucky had advised, to let the dogs do the talking. She created an iMovie filled with photos and videos of the Rescue Rover residents. There was even Trixie gobbling up the pupcake sculpture! Jenna's voice narrated the movie as it played on the classroom SMART Board.

"Rescue Rover is run by Lucille 'Lucky' Gilligan, a lady who gives her heart and soul to saving dogs who have been abused, abandoned, and otherwise forgotten. Rescue Rover is trying to recruit dozens of volunteers from the Connecticut community and to raise funds for everything from training to treats. Lucky's goal is to find every pet at her shelter a loving home."

The last image was a photo Leo had snapped of Jenna snuggling Dulce. "Won't you reach out to a puppy in need? Rescue Rover needs you!" Jenna concluded. The class applauded.

"That was a very moving and heartfelt presentation, Jenna," Ms. Heller commended her. "I can see you really spent a lot of time researching your cause and becoming involved in it."

"Oh, I am." Jenna nodded. "In fact, I'm going back today to visit my puppy."

"I bet it's supersized like her," Meredith muttered under her breath.

Jenna ignored the nasty comment. It was what she did most of the time when Meredith tried to get a rise out of her. But then, she went too far.

"Is it that messy black-and-white thing in the video? What a mutt!" Meredith snickered. "My Fifi comes from a long line of purebred poodles. She's a show dog."

Jenna gritted her teeth. No one—especially not Meredith—was going to call Dulce nasty names.

"If anyone is a messy mutt, it's not Dulce…" Jenna shot back.

Ms. Heller stepped between them. "I'm sure she's a lovely dog. Meredith, kindly keep your opinions to yourself."

"Just sayin'…" Meredith smiled innocently.

"Don't let her ruffle your fur," Ms. Heller whispered to Jenna. "Dulce is absolutely precious."

☆ ☮ ☆

After social studies, Jenna caught up with Kylie in the hallway.

"I know that look," Kylie said, observing the scowl on Jenna's face. "What did Meredith Mitchell do now?"

"She said some totally mean things about Dulce."

"Meredith is picking on an innocent little puppy?" Kylie had dealt with Meredith's mean ways all through fourth grade, and had hoped she'd learned her lesson and stopped bullying. "I guess you can't teach an old dog new tricks. Meredith is always going to have a big mouth."

"Exactly!" Jenna exclaimed. "And if she does it again, it's gonna get ugly. No one messes with my puppy."

Kylie laughed. "You sound like a fierce mommy protecting her young. I've never seen this side of you, Jenna."

Just then, Rodney Higgins, Juliette's boyfriend and Blakely's visiting Shakespeare teacher, ran up to them.

"Girls, can I have a quick word?" he asked. He was looking around anxiously. "You haven't seen Ms. Dubois on this floor of the school, have you?"

Jenna raised an eyebrow. "I think she's teaching second-period drama to the fourth graders downstairs. Why?"

Rodney mopped his brow with a handkerchief. "Oh, phew! That's a relief. I need to ask you a very important favor."

"If you want us to convince Juliette to do a different Shakespeare play next year, it's no-go," Jenna said. "She's determined to do *Macbeth*—even though she says it's not your favorite."

"I prefer *Julius Caesar*—but that's not what I wanted

your help with," he continued. "Can you assure me I have your ultimate confidence?"

Kylie nodded. "If you're asking can we keep a secret… our lips are sealed."

He ushered them into a quiet corner and pulled a small velvet box out of his jacket pocket.

"Is that what I think it is?" Kylie gasped. "A ring?"

"Oh, no…not another engagement!" Jenna groaned. "It's an epidemic! Wedding-itis!"

"I'm afraid so." Rodney blushed. "And you're to blame! If it hadn't been for your fifth-grade Shakespeare class, we would never have met and fallen in love."

Jenna remembered how Rodney and Juliette started off hating each other several months ago, fighting over which actor played the best Hamlet (Juliette thought it was Richard Burton; Rodney thought it was himself) and disagreeing over how to stage the fifth-grade performance of *Romeo and Juliet*. Then one day, as if a bolt of lightning struck them both, everything changed. They started calling each other "sweetheart" and "darling" and staring lovingly into each other's eyes. It was pretty sickening!

Jenna knew her mother and Leo has fallen for each other even quicker than that. Her *mami* called it "*amor a primer vista,*" love at first sight. She insisted that she knew Leo was "The One" before he even spoke a single word. It seemed pretty crazy: how could someone know that in just one look?

But Kylie was a romantic: she believed that Rodney and Juliette, like Romeo and Juliet, were destined to be together, even when they hated each other's guts back in the fall. "We'd love to help, Mr. Higgins," she said. "What did you have in mind?"

"I'd like to place an order for a few dozen cupcakes." Rodney winked.

6

A Nice Ring to It

Back at Kylie's house that afternoon, Jenna admired the beautiful antique sapphire ring that Mr. Higgins had entrusted to them.

"Let me get this straight," Sadie said. "He wants us to hide this engagement ring in the cupcake?"

"It's his grandmother's ring—so it's really special," Kylie explained. "Juliette is gonna flip!"

"Or freak out," Jenna cautioned them. "What if she doesn't feel the same way about Mr. Higgins? What if she doesn't want to marry him?"

"Oh, she will!" Lexi smiled. "If Jeremy gave me an engagement ring in a cupcake, I'd say yes."

"Please…not you too!" Jenna groaned. Lexi and Jeremy Saperstone had been "an item" since they played Romeo and Juliet, but they were both eleven years old! "I can't take one more engagement!"

"Relax," Lexi said, putting an arm around Jenna. "I plan on studying art at Sorbonne University in Paris before I settle down."

"Thank you," Jenna said. "At least someone around here hasn't gone totally crazy."

"What'll we do?" Delaney asked. "How does Mr. Higgins plan on getting Juliette to take a bite?"

Kylie laid out the plan: "We're going to tell Juliette we need to do a taste test of our new spring flavors. We'll tell her we asked Mr. Higgins and Jack Yu to be the other tasters. When she bites into a cupcake and sees something sparkly, Mr. Higgins can pop the question."

Lexi pulled out a list of flavors the club had planned on trying for their spring orders. "I have pink lemonade, mint julep, cherry blossom, peach cobbler, and coconut cream pie."

"Perfect!" Kylie said. "Let's whip 'em up and call a meeting for tomorrow after school. We'll be ready...I hope Mr. Higgins is!"

☆ ☮ ☆

The next day, Kylie passed Jenna in the hall before the last period of the day and gave her a thumbs-up: "Just forty-five minutes 'til Operation I Do!" Honestly, Jenna didn't see what the big deal was. Juliette was perfectly happy being the Blakely drama teacher and their cupcake club advisor. Why did Mr. Higgins have to go and change all of that? She secretly hoped Juliette would reply, "*Gracias*, but no thanks."

Jack and Mr. Higgins came as planned to the PLC meeting. "So are we going to taste some delicious new cupcakes today?" Rodney said, entering the teachers' lounge kitchen. "I'm starving!"

"Wow, he's a pretty good actor," Kylie whispered to Jenna. "I'd never know he was a bundle of nerves, would you?"

"Okay, tasting panel," Kylie announced. "Please jot down your notes on the pads in front of you. Tell us if you think the cupcakes need more or less of something, or if you'd like to see some different decoration. We want your opinions."

Jack raised his hand. "Do I get to eat all the cupcakes?"

"Sure," Lexi answered. "If you'd like to. But save room—there are lots of different ones to taste."

"That's okay," Jack said, rubbing his belly. "I've got plenty of room in here! And I love cupcakes!"

Delaney brought out the first tray with pink lemonade

cupcakes. She and Lexi had created tiny, pink fondant pitchers on top.

"It reminds me of summer," Juliette said, taking a sniff of the lemon-scented frosting. "Did you use zest?"

"Just a tiny bit," Sadie replied. "Is it too much?"

"No, no. It has a sour kick, but I think the sweetness of the cupcake balances it out," Rodney spoke up. "Don't you agree, Jack?"

"What? Huh?" Jack asked. He had gobbled up the cupcake in two bites.

"How did you like it?" Jenna said.

"Oh, it was good. What's the next one?"

The girls brought out tray after tray, and Jenna noticed that Mr. Higgins was starting to lose his cool.

"So, what's your *best* cupcake?" he asked. "Is there one you *really* want Ms. Dubois to taste today?"

"Bring out our *favorite* cupcake," Kylie said, elbowing Delaney.

"I thought I did," she whispered. "Wasn't the ring supposed to be in the mint julep one?"

"I thought you put it in the peach cobbler," Sadie replied.

"Excuse us…" Kylie said, dragging the girls to the corner

of the room. "There will be a brief intermission before the final course."

Juliette looked concerned. "Is everything okay, girls?"

"Great! Fine! Perfect!" Kylie tried to cover.

When they were out of earshot, she handed each girl a pile of toothpicks. "Start poking all the cupcakes till you find that ring!" she said. "Mr. Higgins is going to kill us!"

"I just had a horrible thought," Lexi said, watching Jack lick his fingers. "What if we accidentally gave the cupcake with the ring in it to Jack? He practically inhaled them. What if he ate Juliette's ring?"

Jenna cracked up. "Over the teeth and under the gums, look out, tummy, here it comes!"

"It's not funny, Jenna," Kylie said, gently poking through mounds of frosting.

"Aw, I think it has a nice *ring* to it, don't you?" Jenna joked.

"Wait! Did anyone put nuts in the coconut-cream-pie cupcakes?" Sadie asked.

"No," Kylie answered. "They're supposed to be light and fluffy, no nuts."

"Then I think I found the missing ring," Sadie whispered. They raced over to present the last cupcake tray to the tasters.

"I'm sorry, ladies. I'm stuffed," Juliette said. "And I have costumes to go sew for the second-grade spring festival. I'll take a pass on the last flavor. Jack and Rodney can give you their verdict." She pushed her plate away and started to get up from the table.

"Wait! No!" Kylie shouted. "We really need you to taste this one!" She looked nervously at Jenna and mouthed, "Help me!"

"Right. This is the best one," Jenna improvised. "I used a rare blend of shredded coconut…from Canada."

Juliette looked skeptical. "Canada? Don't coconuts grow on palm trees in the tropics?"

"That's what makes this coconut so rare," Jenna continued. "It's called the Coco Canadian. And since you're from Canada, Juliette, you're the only one who can really tell us if it tastes, um, authentic."

"Absolutely!" Mr. Higgins added. "I defer to Ms. Dubois on this cupcake."

Juliette looked at the cupcake: it seemed normal enough. Lexi had created a delicate meringue frosting to hide what was really inside.

"Okay, I'll take one bite," Juliette said. She poked at the cupcake gingerly with her fork before digging in. "It's good.

Very moist. Very fresh. I think your Canadian Coconut is a hit, Jenna."

"What? That's all?" Kylie cried. "What about what's inside?"

Juliette was puzzled. "I don't taste any filling. Am I missing something?"

Mr. Higgins suddenly grabbed the cupcake and mashed it on the table with his fist. There was no ring.

"Rodney!" Juliette gasped. "What are you doing?" Frosting and crumbs went flying everywhere. He started sniffing the plate like a hunting dog.

"It…must…be…here…" he stammered, digging through the frosting.

"If you didn't like the flavor, you didn't have to destroy it!" Juliette exclaimed. "What's come over you?"

"I didn't love it either," Jack said. "Mine was kinda lumpy."

"Lumpy?" Jenna asked. "Gimme your plate." She seized the cupcake out of Jack's hands.

"Hey!" he protested. "I didn't say I was done with it! I'm still hungry!"

Jenna used a fork to pick through the remaining cupcake half on his plate. There, on the very bottom of the wrapper, was the sapphire ring.

She handed it to Mr. Higgins, who was frantically trying to explain his strange behavior to Juliette. "I think your cupcake was missing an important ingredient," Jenna said, handing the ring to Juliette.

"What's this?" Juliette asked.

Mr. Higgins got down on one knee and recited his favorite lines from Shakespeare's *The Tempest*: "Hear my soul speak: The very instant that I saw you, did my heart fly to your service." Then he took a deep breath, looked into Juliette's eyes, and asked, "Will you marry me?"

Juliette was speechless. Here it comes, thought Jenna. She's going to turn him down. No one said a word. They just waited.

Finally, Rodney spoke. "I know it was a crumby proposal...literally." He dusted the cupcake crumbs off his shirt. "I wanted it to be perfect."

"It was totally our fault," Kylie added. "Please don't blame Mr. Higgins. We mixed up the cupcakes. We ruined everything."

"Nonsense!" Juliette insisted. "It was the sweetest thing anyone has ever done for me."

"Does that mean you're saying yes?" Rodney asked.

Jenna could see the beads of sweat on his brow and the tears in Juliette's eyes.

"Yes! Yes! Yes!" Juliette cried and kissed him. Everyone cheered—even Jenna. But Juliette could see the concern on her face.

"Don't worry, Jenna," she said. "We won't be getting married in a month. We both have the school year to finish out before we think about walking down the aisle."

"Will you get married in Vegas too?" Delaney asked.

"Oh, no! Canada where my family is," Juliette replied.

"Really, darling? I was thinking more of London where I hail from," Rodney said.

"No, sweetheart," Juliette said, patting her fiancé's hand. "You know I always dreamed of getting married at the Chateau Frontenac in Quebec."

"But, Buttercup." Rodney smiled sweetly. "What about the Barbican Centre Conservatory in London? It doesn't get more theatrical than that."

"Some things never change, I guess," Kylie said, shaking her head. "You two will always disagree."

"It's called having strong opinions," Rodney replied. "And it's one of the reasons I love Ms. Dubois. She challenges me!"

Juliette blushed. "Aw, I love you too. We can get married in London if it means that much to you."

"No, no, no," Rodney countered. "You're right. The Chateau is magical. Canada it is."

"Guys, guys!" Jack suddenly interrupted. "Can we talk about this later? Bring out the rest of the cupcakes. I'm still hungry."

7

Bridesmaids and Bunnies

The weeks flew by, and Jenna continued visiting Dulce and the other dogs at Rescue Rover as often as Leo or Marisol would drive her to Danbury. But there was so much to be done in such a short amount of time for the wedding: invitations, dress fittings, floral arrangements, even finding someone to officiate the ceremony.

"What about this one?" Gabby suggested, showing her mother a wedding chapel she had googled on her phone. "It's called Viva Las Vegas—and instead of limos, we ride to the ceremony in pink Cadillacs!"

"*Dios mío!*" her mother said, looking at the photo. "That is not for me! My *mami* is coming all the way from Ecuador. I want *una ceremonia de la boda* that is less—how do you say it?" She tried to find the right word in English.

"Tacky? Obnoxious? Disgusting?" Jenna offered.

"I think your mother is trying to say she wants our

wedding ceremony to be *dignified*," Leo said. "Whatever she wants is okay by me. Although I agree, Gabby—that pink Caddy rocks."

It was Kylie's suggestion to contact the hotel about using their kitchen to bake the wedding cupcakes.

"We're all set," Jenna told the girls. "We arrive Saturday at two p.m., and we can hit the kitchen by four. The concierge says there's a small one that they use for event catering, and it's all ours for as long as we need it. We just email them a list of ingredients and they'll stock them."

"How long is it going to take us?" asked Delaney. "That's a ton of cupcakes."

Sadie raised her hand. "Let me do the math—I need some practice before my algebra test next week." She jotted down the figures. "We know we have to bake fourteen dozen cupcakes—plus the giant one on the top tier…"

"And the oven will hold four dozen at a time," Jenna explained.

"So we can bake four dozen every thirty minutes if we get crackin' on the batter," Sadie continued. "So we'll need at least two hours to get all those cupcakes baked."

"Figure in another fifteen minutes per batch to cool and at least another hour to frost them," Lexi said. "I'll also need at least an hour to decorate the giant cupcake—I want a Cornelli lace pattern on the sides and carnations on top. Delaney can handle the fondant monogram while I pipe."

"And the giant cupcake will take over an hour to bake through," Kylie reminded her. "Remember last time when we made that giant Christmas tree cupcake for my dad's holiday office party, and it was mushy in the middle?"

"It wasn't mushy," Delaney defended her creation. "It was just a little overly moist…"

Sadie held up her sheet filled with calculations. "We're looking at six hours to be safe for baking and decorating. I don't see how we can do it any faster."

"Which means it will be ten p.m. before we even can start building the tower." Jenna sighed. "It's gonna be a long, long night."

☆ ☮ ☆

The cupcake club was used to pulling all-nighters— especially on holidays and for special occasions. Kylie made sure that every single one of the Easter orders were delivered on the Friday before Easter.

"Let's get hoppin'," she said, packing up dozens of

cupcakes for the Golden Spoon's order. "I promised Mr. Ludwig we'd deliver no later than five p.m."

"These are so adorable," Delaney said, admiring the V.I.Peeps cupcakes they'd made with marshmallow chicks on top. "Mr. Ludwig is going to love these."

"I like the little lambs Lexi made out of mini marshmal-lows," Sadie said. "This is our best Easter yet."

"And our busiest," Kylie reminded them. "As soon as your brothers get back with the last batch of orders for delivery, there are twenty more that need to go out."

Jenna was glad that things were so hectic. It kept her mind off leaving tomorrow for Las Vegas.

"You must be so excited," Delaney said. "I am—and it's not even my mom getting married."

"I don't want to think about it," Jenna said. She popped a mini marshmallow in her mouth. "So some-*bunny* change the subject."

"How about this," Kylie said, waving an order form in her hands. "We just got an emergency email from Principal Fontina. She wants a dozen Easter cat cupcakes for her Sunday brunch party."

"Easter cats? Who ever heard of Easter cats?" Lexi said. "I've heard of bunnies, chicks, and lambs...but cats?"

"She's the principal—don't argue with her!" Sadie said. "If she wants Easter monkeys, give 'em to her! I'm barely passing math—I need all the brownie points I can get."

"You mean cupcake points." Kylie corrected her. "We can do some cute little kitties with pastel bows and put them on top of our basic Easter dozen."

"I guess she's a cat person," Jenna shrugged. "I'm a dog person myself." Thinking about Dulce alone on Easter morning made her sad. She would have gone and brought the puppy a little pupcake and a bunny chew toy if it weren't for the stupid wedding.

"Mom, we have a Cupcake 911!" Kylie called from the kitchen. Her mother was on deadline writing an article for a magazine—something about the latest bagless vacuum cleaners and how they were better for the environment.

"Kylie, I told you—I'm chained to my desk this afternoon," her mom answered.

"But we have to get these over to Principal Fontina."

"No can do, honey," her mom said. "I've got five hundred more words to write, and I've run out of ways to describe dirt and dust."

"My bros are both out on orders, and my dad is on a contracting job," Sadie said. "So we don't have any cars."

"Ugh," Jenna said. "I think I know someone we can call…"

☆ ☮ ☆

Ten minutes later, Leo rang the Carsons' doorbell. "Cupcake Delivery Man at your service," he said, standing at attention. "You bake it…I bring it. Where to?"

"Blakely Elementary…and step on it," Jenna said, placing the cupcakes in the trunk. She and Sadie piled into the backseat.

"Thanks so much for saving us, Mr. Winters," Sadie said. "I know Principal Fontina will be very grateful. Hopefully grateful enough to overlook my last test score for my report card…"

"It's Leo…and you're welcome," he said, hitting the gas pedal. "Hold on, girls. I'll have you there in a jiffy."

"Jiffy?" Sadie whispered to Jenna.

"Don't ask." Jenna slumped in her seat. "He's weird."

When they arrived at Blakely, Principal Fontina had her coat on and was waiting at the door to leave. "Here ya go!" Sadie said, handing the box to her. "Just what you asked for: a dozen Easter cat cupcakes."

"Easter cat? Whoever heard of an Easter cat?" their principal said. "I emailed Kylie for a dozen Easter *hat* cupcakes. You know…like people wear in the Easter Parade?"

Jenna took out a printout of the email and double-checked it. "Nope. You wrote Easter cats—as in meow, meow." She showed the principal the paper.

"I hate typing on this new phone," Principal Fontina sighed. "I'm always making typos. I know it's my fault, but how am I supposed to serve Easter cat cupcakes for dessert Sunday?"

"Well," Jenna improvised, "you can say they're the 'purrfect' treat for Easter?"

Principal Fontina mulled it over. "That's very clever…"

"And why not serve them with a side of 'mousemallow' topping…" Jenna continued.

"Brilliant!" Principal Fontina replied, taking the box and hurrying on her way. "I can't wait to see my guests' faces."

☆ ☮ ☆

When they got back in the car, Sadie hugged Jenna. "Did anyone ever tell you you're a genius?" she said. "You seriously saved our butts. I was afraid she'd make us stay after school for messing up her order."

"Did she like the cupcakes?" Leo asked.

"Like them? She loved them!" Sadie replied. "Thanks to Jenna's quick thinking."

Jenna wished she could come up with an equally brilliant solution to get her mother to cancel the wedding. But it was no use: Leo was determined.

"Now that all your Easter orders are delivered, you girls can relax and get ready for *la boda del año*—the wedding of the year!" he said.

8

Viva Las Vegas

Jenna had never seen anything like Las Vegas. On the "strip" where all the hotels were located, everything was all flashing lights and video screens advertising everything from circus shows, roller coasters, and star-studded concerts to all-you-can-eat buffets. Each hotel had a different theme and was modeled after a different place: Paris, New York, Egypt, even Caesar's Palace.

But the Venice Hotel looked like something out of a fairy tale. As she strolled through the lobby, Jenna noticed the soaring arches, towering columns, breathtaking artwork, and elaborate gold sculptures. The ceiling of the resort was painted to look like the sky, complete with fluffy white clouds and cherubs. In the center of the main palazzo was a replica of the Grand Canal with gondolas gliding on the water.

"Wow." She whistled through her teeth. "This place is amazing."

"It feels like we're in a different world," Kylie exclaimed. "Look at all the cafes—and the jugglers and artists."

Delaney grabbed Jenna's mother around the waist and hugged her. "Thank you," she squealed. "Thank you for getting married here. I feel like Alice in Wonderland!"

Ms. Medina and Leo went to check in, leaving Marisol and Gabby in charge.

"All of you stay with me," Marisol commanded. "That means you, Manny…" He was already trying to figure out how to sneak into the casino filled with lights and noise. A security guard stopped him in his tracks.

"See this sign? No one allowed under twenty-one," the guard said.

Manny scratched his chin. "I'm in kindergarten. I don't read," he replied.

The guard chuckled. "Well, then I'll just make it real easy for you. Anywhere you see this uniform…you don't go."

Manny nodded, but Jenna knew it would take a lot more than that to keep her mischievous little brother away from the clanking slot machines. The casino looked like a giant video arcade.

"Manny, if you want to be in the wedding, you have

to behave yourself," she instructed. "No wandering off, *comprende?*"

Of course, that didn't apply to the PLC girls who had already taken off with Gabby to explore the hotel's palazzo. Lexi perched herself on a stool so she could watch an artisan sculpt a bust. "I can't believe how amazing his technique is," she whispered, watching him chisel away at the lump of plaster to create an image of a woman.

"Do me next! Do me next!" Ricky shouted.

Gabby caught him by the hand. "That would require sitting still—which you never do," she said.

"I wanna go swimming in the pool!" Ricky suddenly shouted, spying a giant water fountain.

"*Dios mío!* It's not a pool…it's a fountain!" Gabby cried, chasing after him before he could leap into the water.

"I think they think this hotel is an amusement park," Jenna sighed. "Maybe you can take them to the real pool on the roof and keep them out of trouble?"

Gabby pouted. "What about me? When do I get to shop and walk around? How come I have to babysit?"

Jenna's face grew stern. "Because I'm the one who has to do all the baking for Mami's wedding. Would you rather be slaving over a hot oven for six hours?"

Gabby thought it over. "Fine. You win. Marisol and I will take the Terror Twins." She glanced over at Ricky, who was trying to fish coins out of the fountain. Manny had caught up to him and was holding his brother's ankles so he wouldn't fall in.

"No!" Gabby and Marisol screamed, then called behind them, "Jenna, you owe us!"

Kylie was also anxious to rein in her PLC mates and get them focused on the job at hand. "We'll have lots of time to check the place out after we finish the cupcakes," she pleaded. "Guys? Please?"

Sadie was fascinated by a stilt walker roaming the "streets" of Venice. "I've never seen someone that tall," she said. "We could sure use you for the Blakely Bears basketball team."

Delaney was equally mesmerized, but by the gondoliers singing Italian songs as they paddled the long, narrow boats through the canal. "When the moon hits your eye like a big pizza pie, that's *amore*!" they sang.

Jenna knew exactly how to get everyone's attention. She placed two fingers between her teeth and blew a deafening whistle. Lexi, Delaney, and Sadie all jumped.

"*Escúchame*, listen up!" she said. "My *mami* is getting

married in the morning. We'll have plenty of time to check the place out after we get the cupcakes baked and decorated."

"She's right," Kylie said. "Let's find the concierge and get to the kitchen."

They wandered back through the lobby where they found a man impeccably dressed in a black suit and red tie. "Excuse me," Jenna began. "We're Peace, Love, and Cupcakes, and we have permission from the catering manager to use one of your kitchens."

No sooner had she gotten the words out than a voice behind her barged in. "Excuse me, did you say you're bakers? Lordy, I'm in luck!"

Jenna spun around and had to blink twice to make sure she wasn't imagining the figure in front of her. He was dressed in a gold lamé jumpsuit covered in sequins and wore long sideburns and sunglasses.

"I know you!" Delaney cried. "You're the King of Rock and Roll! You're Elvis!"

"In the flesh." The man bowed deeply. "Thank you very much."

"You mean, he's an Elvis impersonator," Jenna corrected her. "They're all over Vegas. Come on, guys, we have to get baking."

"Wait! Please!" Elvis insisted. "It's my hundredth show here at the hotel and I need a cake," he pleaded with the girls. "I've called every bakery in Vegas, and no one can do it on such short notice. I was just coming to the concierge to ask for his help, and lo and behold, you girls came along! Now is that destiny or what?"

"What," Jenna grumped.

Lexi was curious: "A cake should be pretty easy to find. Why would everyone tell you no?"

"Because it has to be the King's favorite flavor: peanut butter banana."

Kylie nodded. "Yup, I can see how that could be a problem. Not just any baker can do PBB."

"And it needs to serve my entire audience at tonight's show," Elvis added. "All 250 of them."

Jenna tugged on Kylie's arm. "The kitchen's this way. Let's go. Sorry, Elvis, can't help you. Adios!"

As Jenna turned to leave, Elvis started singing. A crowd gathered around them, and they were trapped. "I'm all shook up! Uh-huh, yeah!" he sang, shaking his hips.

"He's pretty good," Delaney said. "I'm impressed."

"And it would be kind of fun to do Elvis cupcakes," Lexi added. "It's very Vegas."

Kylie put it to a vote. "All in favor of helping out the King?" Kylie said. She, Sadie, Delaney, and Lexi raised their hands. Only Jenna was against it.

"I just don't think we have time with all the preparations that need to be done for the wedding," Jenna pointed out.

"I'll pay you double what you normally charge per cupcake," Elvis insisted.

"Did you hear that? Double!" Sadie whispered.

"I can make some fondant records, guitars, and musical notes—maybe even blue suede shoes—to put on top of the cupcakes," Lexi said. "It'll be okay, Jenna. We can divide the work up between us."

Kylie left it up to Jenna. "What do you say?"

"Fine…I give up!" Jenna said. "You win, Elvis. We'll deliver 250 cupcakes to your show tonight." She handed him a PLC business card.

"Thank you, thank you very much," Elvis replied. "You ladies better rock and roll if you want to make my eight p.m. performance."

9

Cupcakes Fit for The King

The kitchen was huge and fancy—just like the rest of the Venice Hotel. There were an industrial mixer, an enormous commercial oven, and tons of baking supplies—everything Jenna had asked the catering manager to get them. But it took the girls over an hour just to hunt down all the ingredients they needed and get them organized.

"I never thought I'd miss my *mami*'s tiny kitchen," Jenna said, climbing on a step stool to search for salt in a cabinet. "At least I know where everything is. This is way too big and way too confusing."

Sadie walked around, checking things off on their list. "We have condensed milk, evaporated milk, and coconut milk—that's the *tres leches*."

"I'm worried about the butter and sugar," Jenna said. "With all we need for the Elvis order, we might run short."

Kylie did a quick tally. "I'm more worried about how many bananas we need for the King's cupcakes."

Jenna shook her head: this was a disaster—and she couldn't even blame it on Manny and Ricky. "I think Lexi, Sadie, and Delaney should start on the batters while Kylie and I go borrow some supplies from a few of the restaurants in the hotel."

"Bring us back some snacks," Sadie called after them.

"Pizza!" Delaney added. "Extra cheese and pepperoni. And some garlic knots...and meatballs! Gosh, I love Venice!"

They borrowed flour from an Italian pizzeria, sugar from a gelato shop, and bananas from an Italian bakery. They could barely carry all the ingredients and the two large pizzas back to the kitchen.

When they returned, the mixer was whirring and there were already two batches of *tres leches* cupcakes baking in the oven.

"It smells like heaven in here!" Kylie exclaimed.

Sadie grabbed a pizza out of her hands. "No, *this* smells like heaven! I'm starving."

They gobbled up the slices and started on the batter for the Elvis show.

"I think we should do our signature banana cake and

top it with peanut butter frosting and a little marshmallow fluff," Lexi suggested. "I can start right away coloring the fondant to make the toppers."

Delaney searched the albums on her iPod until she found her fave Elvis tune. "You ain't nothing but a hound dog, cryin' all the time!" she sang, strumming her spoon like a guitar.

"You ain't nothin' but a hound dog," Jenna chimed in. But the mention of the word *dog* made her suddenly sad as she remembered her little Dulce puppy at the shelter. Was the little dog waiting for her every day at the window? Was she wondering where and why Jenna had disappeared for the past several days? Jenna felt so guilty—Dulce always looked forward to her visits and greeted her with wet puppy kisses.

Kylie read her friend's mind. "I'm sure she's fine, and you can see her when you get home."

Jenna nodded. "Yes, but that doesn't make me miss her any less right now."

"You know what I think?" Lexi told her, expertly piping a purple G clef on one of the cupcakes. "It was love at first sight. You saw Dulce, and you were struck by lightning—just like Juliette and Rodney, and your mom and Leo."

Jenna thought about it. Maybe it wasn't so crazy after all. She couldn't get the tiny puppy out of her mind or her heart.

"You think that's how my *mami* feels about Leo?" she asked. She'd never considered that. She thought her mom had just rushed into the relationship without giving it much thought.

"For sure!" Kylie said. "Do you see how her face lights up every time Leo walks in the room? It's so sweet. They really love each other. They want to be together. It's just like you feel about Dulce."

"Done!" Lexi declared, placing the last sprinkling of luster dust on the cupcakes to make them glitter. "You guys can go take these to Elvis. Sadie, Delaney, and I will start frosting and stacking the wedding tower."

Lexi had arranged the cupcakes on a rolling cart to spell out *ELVIS*.

"We better hurry," Kylie said, checking the time. "We have only five minutes 'til curtain!"

They raced through the hotel lobby, weaving in and out of guests until they reached the stage door. A man was peering out, looking anxious.

"Finally!" he shouted when he saw them. "Do you

know what time it is? He's been waiting for these. Go right out onstage."

Jenna gulped. "Onstage? You want us to go onstage?"

"Yes, yes," he said, pushing them and the cart in the direction of the wings. "Hurry up. Show's starting!"

Jenna and Kylie looked at each other. "He didn't say anything about us being part of his act," Kylie whispered. "I'm a mess! There's peanut butter stuck to my hair!"

But it was too late. A loud voice boomed across the theater: "Ladies and gentlemen, put your hands together for the one, the only, the King of Rock and Roll, Elvis Presley!"

A trapdoor in the stage opened and smoke rolled out. Elvis rose out of the floor dressed in a white jumpsuit studded with gold. On the back of his white cape was an eagle, beaded in sequins. As the crowd went wild, he began singing, "Bright light city gonna set my soul, gonna set my soul on fire!" Fireworks suddenly exploded behind him spelling out "ELVIS" in balls of fire.

"OMG!" Kylie gasped. "This is crazy!"

"Get out there! Get out there!" the stage manager barked at them. "What are you waiting for?"

"A fire extinguisher?" Jenna quipped.

He pushed the cart of cupcakes, sending it speeding

toward the center of the stage. Jenna and Kylie chased after it and stopped it just before it ran Elvis over.

"Viva Las Vegas! Viva Las Vegas!" Elvis sang, dancing around them.

Jenna and Kylie froze. The audience was on its feet, clapping and singing along.

"Thank you, thank you very much," Elvis said, mopping the sweat from his forehead with a silk scarf. He threw it to Jenna.

"Eww!" she screamed. "Gross!"

"You know when I started in this business, I was an itty-bitty guy with an itty-bitty guitar and itty-bitty sideburns. Then the Venice Hotel put me onstage," he said. "And tonight, I am celebrating my hundredth performance!"

The crowd screamed again.

"And to help me celebrate with all of you tonight, these lovely ladies have made me some amazing cupcakes in my favorite flavor: peanut butter banana. My helpers are gonna hand these out to everyone in the audience." Two Vegas showgirls dressed in sequins and feathers appeared from the wings with silver platters.

"Give it up for Peace, Love, and Cupcakes!" Elvis shouted.

"Woo-hoo!" the crowd roared. "We love you!"

"Do they mean us…or Elvis?" Jenna joked.

"Take a bow, ladies, take a bow!" Elvis said. "You deserve it!"

☆ ☮ ☆

When they got back to the kitchen, Lexi was standing on a ladder, trying to stack cupcakes on each of the tiers.

"You guys won't believe what happened to us!" Kylie reported. "Elvis dragged us out onstage with him…and there was fire…and smoke…and sequins."

"Shhh!" Lexi hushed her. "This takes complete concentration and silence." She was delicately piping lines on each cupcake 'til the frosting on top looked like lace. "Hand me the candy pearls, Delaney," she whispered. "Carefully!"

"Don't breathe," Sadie instructed Kylie and Jenna. "The artist is at work."

Lexi frowned. "Did you see that sculptor working on that bust in the palazzo? He would not stand for any distractions."

"Like I said," Sadie whispered. "She's in the zone. Shhh…"

"What can we do?" Jenna asked.

Delaney handed her a rolling pin. "Roll fondant. My hands are killing me."

By 11:30 p.m., the tower was complete, all except for the giant cupcake on top.

"My eyes are closing," Lexi groaned. "I can't pipe one more drop line or I'll drop."

"We could get up early tomorrow, say six a.m., before we have to get dressed for the wedding," Kylie suggested.

Jenna nodded. "I think we take a break." There were bits and pieces of gum paste stuck to her face, her hands, even her sneakers, and frosting, flour, and sugar coated her shirt and jeans. "A little more fondant, and I could be the giant cupcake on top."

10

Too Hot to Handle

Jenna's wake-up call rang at exactly 5 a.m.

"Good morning!" said a chipper voice from the reception desk. "This is your five o'clock wake-up call."

"Ugh," Jenna yawned. "Could ya not be so happy about it?"

"It's a beautiful day!" the woman continued. "Lots of bright sunshine and temperatures in the 90s."

"Did you say 90s?" Jenna was suddenly wide awake.

"Yes, we're expecting a bit of a heat wave for April—103 degrees by noon."

"*Dios mío!*" Jenna slammed the receiver down. "We have a huge *problema*!"

She raced through the suite and into the other bedroom where the girls were fast asleep. "Kylie, Sadie, Lexi, Delaney—*despierta*! Wake up!"

Kylie rubbed her eyes. "What's the matter?"

"It's supposed to be over 100 degrees today! Our cupcakes are gonna be soup in that sun!" Jenna said, tugging off their comforters. "We need a Plan B, fast!"

"Why didn't you think about the cupcakes melting before?" Lexi complained.

"Who knew we were gonna have a heat wave?" Jenna cried.

"Calm down." Kylie tried to be the voice of reason. "We can keep the cupcake tower indoors until dessert, in the air-conditioned lobby. Maybe set up some fans to blow on it outside when we wheel it into the garden?"

"Okay, okay." Jenna tried to steady her nerves. "Maybe that will work."

Delaney raised her hand. "Guys. Just one question: Didn't we shut off all the power in the kitchen last night when we left?"

"Yes," Kylie said. "We turned off all the power like we were supposed to."

"*Including the air conditioner!*" Jenna screamed. "Double dios mio!" The girls raced through the lobby, still in their pj's, and unlocked the door to the kitchen.

"It's like an oven in here," Jenna said. "It must be 100 degrees!" She flipped on the light, and there was the cupcake tower, looking wilted.

Lexi climbed the ladder and inspected each tier. "Oh, no! All the icing is mush!" she said. "It all melted." She handed Jenna a cupcake with a sad little puddle of royal icing on top.

"Let's not panic," Kylie said.

Lexi nodded. "Fondant is gum paste. It will hold up better than icing. We can put a layer of buttercream under it."

"And we rolled out tons of it last night and put it in the fridge," Delaney said.

Kylie held up her cell phone. "Check this out. This is called the giant granadilla flower, and it's native to Ecuador." She showed her friends a large, white and purple blossom with intricate fringe petals. "That would cover each cupcake and look really pretty."

"*Sí*," Jenna said. "I saw those in Ecuador. "They're called the passion flower because they give off passion fruit. That would be perfect for a wedding."

"We could do a passion fruit buttercream under the fondant," Sadie added. "That would be delicious with the *tres leches* cake."

Kylie looked at the clock on the oven. "Guys, I don't want to scare you, but we have only three hours 'til we have to be dressed and ready for photos in the garden."

"Move! Move!" Jenna shouted. "Sadie and Kylie, you're on the buttercream; Lexi and Delaney, you do the granadillas, and I'll scrape off the mess on all these cupcakes!" They set the kitchen table up like an assembly line in a factory: Jenna scraped; Sadie spread on a thin layer of buttercream; Lexi and Delaney decorated. Kylie stood at the end and stacked each cupcake on the tower tiers. "Keep it comin,'" she called. "Only about 150 more to go!"

"*Qué desastre!*" Jenna panted, scraping the cupcakes as fast as she could with a flat knife. "What a mess!"

It took them two hours, but by 7:30 a.m., all of the cupcakes were done except the giant one on top.

"Let's cover it in white fondant and figure out what to place on top as a decoration," Lexi said.

Delaney rolled the gum paste smooth and thin, and Kylie helped her lower it gently over the cupcake.

"It's a big blank cupcake," Jenna said. "Now what?"

"I'm thinking! I'm thinking!" Lexi replied, frazzled. "I was going to do the monogram on a white chocolate plaque, but that would melt in the heat."

"We can't just have a big white cupcake—it'll look awful in pictures," Delaney said.

"Pictures! Delaney, that's it! You're a genius!" Jenna cried.

She dug in her purse and pulled out the wedding invitation with a photo of her mother and Leo on it.

"What won't melt in the heat? A sculpture! You watched that artist sculpt a figure in the palazzo yesterday that was amazing. Let's go find him and see if he'll do one of my mom and Leo fast!"

"That's brilliant," Lexi said. "We can put a dowel through the center of the cupcake to support it on top, and it will be an amazing keepsake for your mom and stepdad."

Jenna and Kylie were already out the door, racing through the Venice streets in search of the Italian sculptor. They found him setting up his wares on a table next to the gondola ride.

"Sir! Sir!" Jenna cried. "Can you come with me—and bring your tools and some plaster? We need you to sculpt a bride and groom for a wedding cake!"

"*Che cosa?*" the man asked.

"Oh, no!" Jenna replied. "Do you speak English? *Habla español?*"

"*Non capisco,*" the man tried to explain.

"I don't speak Italian, but I'm pretty sure that means, 'I have no idea what you are saying,'" Kylie said.

"Wait! I know someone who *does* speak Italian!" Jenna said. "Stay here!" she told the artist. "Don't move!"

She raced upstairs to the penthouse bridal suite and banged on the door. "Leo, Leo! Come quick! We need you!" she shouted.

Leo came to the door, already in his tuxedo. "What's up, Jenna? Everything okay? Your mom went to get ready with your sisters and brothers…"

"That's great—we don't want them to see," Kylie added.

"See what?" Leo asked.

Jenna grabbed his hand. "Don't ask questions. Just come with us!" They ran back to the artist who looked frightened that they had returned.

"Tell him we need him to make a sculpture of a bride and groom," Jenna told Leo.

"*Signore*," Leo began. He explained what the girls needed, and that it was an "*emergenza*."

"Well?" Jenna asked. "Will he do it?"

"*Sì, sì*." The man smiled. He picked up his chisel and a small block of plaster.

Jenna grabbed the startled gentleman by the arm. "Come with me! Quick!"

Leo chuckled. "Try '*Venga subito*' and he'll understand

you better. And I'll see you at the wedding, girls, in two hours—hopefully out of your pajamas."

☆ ☮ ☆

The finished sculpture looked exactly like Jenna's mother and Leo. "It's amazing," Jenna said, admiring it. "How can we ever thank you?"

He held out his hand. "400 *dollari*."

Sadie searched for an Italian translation on her phone. "He just asked you for 400 dollars."

"No way! That's all the profit we made on the Elvis cupcakes!" Kylie said.

Jenna handed over a stack of twenty-dollar bills. "Here ya go. So much for making money this weekend."

"*Grazie*," the artist said, tipping his cap. "*Buongiorno*."

"At least we have an amazing cupcake tower for your mom's wedding," Kylie said. "And twenty minutes to get dressed and cleaned up."

Something Borrowed

The garden gazebo at the Venice Hotel was decorated with dozens of white roses and swags of lace.

Jenna stood outside on the balcony of the bridal suite, taking it all in. The guests were already beginning to file in and take their seats. She spotted her grandma and her aunt and uncle from Ecuador, as well as her cousins. There were also tons of fashionable men and women that she assumed were Leo's Ralph Warren colleagues.

The suite was abuzz with activity: Gabby and Marisol were arguing over whether to wear their hair up or down; Ricky and Manny were fighting over the TV in the living room; and the PLC girls were primping in the bathroom.

"What are you doing out here?" Kylie asked, stepping out onto the balcony. She was dressed in the gold taffeta dress Jenna's mom had sewn for all the junior brides-maids. It had a sweetheart neck and a puffy skirt with crinoline underneath, and the neckline fell softly around her shoulders.

"You look beautiful," Jenna said.

"So do you!" Kylie gasped. "Spin! Let me see!"

Jenna's dress was extraspecial: a cream-colored taffeta with a gold sash around the waist and pearls adorning the bodice. Her mother had made small cap sleeves out of lace to match the bridal veil.

"OMG! You're gorgeous!" Kylie gushed.

"Of course I am," Jenna joked. "Gorgeous is my middle name."

"Actually, it's Alanza—which means 'ready for battle,'" her sister Marisol interrupted. "Very fitting, don't you think, for my little sis who always has a chip on her shoulder?"

Marisol's and Gabby's gowns were floor-length and strapless but had the same pearl and gold sash detail as Jenna's. "You should come say hi to Leo's daughter, Maggie. She's here," Marisol told her.

"Great." Jenna sighed. "I can hardly wait."

Maggie was chatting with Lexi, Sadie, and Delaney—something about Lady Gaga coming in concert in the spring to NYC. Jenna had met her once or twice, but never thought she'd become her stepsister. It felt strange to think of yet another kid in the Medina family.

"Hey, Jenna!" Delaney called. "We're all gonna get tix to see Gaga in concert! Maggie's a big fan too."

"I'm not gaga over Gaga," Jenna replied.

"You look really nice," Maggie told her. "Your mom is an amazing dress designer. Our dad says maybe she can come work with him at Ralph Warren."

Jenna winced as Maggie said "*our* dad," but put it out of her mind. She wouldn't ruin things for her mom, no matter how she felt.

A hush suddenly fell over the suite as her mother strolled out in her wedding dress. The top was completely covered in lace and pearls, and the skirt fell in soft ruffled layers to the floor. Her head was covered with a traditional mantilla, a lace shawl that draped gently over her head and shoulders. "This belonged to your *abuela*," she said. "It's something old."

"And your earrings are borrowed from me," Marisol said. "My favorite pearl studs."

"And your dress is something new—since you made it," Gabby chimed in. "So all that's left is something blue."

Maggie walked over and handed her new stepmom a velvet pouch. "I think this might work," she said. In it was a silver heart-shaped locket with the letter *B* for "Betty" spelled out in tiny blue sapphires. "I thought you could put a photo of you and Leo in it."

"*Que linda!* It's perfect," Jenna's mom said, hugging Maggie. Once again, Jenna flinched.

"It was really sweet of Maggie to get her a gift," Lexi whispered to Jenna. "She's really nice."

"Uh-huh," Jenna brushed off her comment. "Where are the bouquets? Why aren't they here yet?"

"They are," Kylie said. "Which is our surprise for you, Jenna." She handed Jenna a box. Inside was a bouquet made out of mini cupcakes, covered in white and gold fondant. "It was your mom's idea for all the bridesmaids. A little PLC personal touch!"

Lexi handed Jenna's mom her bouquet: each of the cupcakes was decorated with a white fondant rose. "*Te gusta*, Jenna? Do you like it?"

"I love it." Jenna smiled.

"Now all we're waiting on is the *juez de paz*, the justice of the peace, to arrive," Marisol said, checking the time. He was more than thirty minutes late. Leo had just sent her a text saying the guests were all melting in the scorching midday sun. Where was he?

"I tried his cell phone—there's no answer," Gabby whispered to her.

"*Qué? Dónde está?*" Their mother was starting to fret. "We can't get married without someone to marry us!"

They waited and waited…'til the guests were wilting and the ceremony was almost an hour delayed.

"Where did you find this guy?" Jenna whispered to Gabby.

"Wed-in-vegas.com," Gabby replied. "It was him, Liberace, or the Elvis guy who performs here at the hotel."

"Elvis? Elvis is a justice of the peace?" Jenna gasped.

"I guess so," Gabby said. "Why?"

"Mami, get ready to walk down the aisle." Jenna beamed. "There's someone who owes us a big favor…"

With This Cupcake, I Thee Wed

As the harpist played Elvis's "I Can't Help Falling in Love with You," a white carpet rolled down the pathway to the garden gazebo. Ricky and Manny were the first to walk down it and only punched each other half the time. Sadie, Lexi, Delaney, and Kylie followed in pairs, then Marisol and Gabby and Maggie and Jenna, each carrying a cupcake bouquet.

Finally, the audience rose to their feet, and the bridal march began to play. Jenna watched as her mother slowly walked down the aisle, smiling nervously. She met Leo under the canopy of roses and stared at the person presiding over the ceremony. It was Elvis, dressed in his finest crystal-studded white leather jumpsuit.

"*Ay, dios mío!*" Jenna's mom said, but Leo held her hand tightly and smiled. "It'll be fine, Betty."

"Dearly beloved," Elvis began. "We are gathered here

today because Leo asked Betty, 'Will You Love Me Tender?' and she agreed…"

"Oh, boy." Jenna gulped. "I hope Elvis doesn't overdo it."

"I know these two love each other with all their hearts," Elvis continued. "I can see it in their eyes. And I know how much their children love them as well." He looked over at Jenna. "They'd do anything for you. Even wake Elvis up before noon."

He motioned for Ricky to bring him the wedding rings on a pillow. "Come here, little fella."

Ricky shook his head and stomped his foot. "Not unless you give me your sunglasses," he insisted.

"*Dar ahora!*" Jenna gritted her teeth. "Give it to him now!" She would have pounced on him and wrestled the pillow out of his hand, but Kylie was holding her back.

"Sure, I'll give you my cool, one of a kind King of Rock and Roll glasses for those rings," Elvis said, making the trade. He handed the first ring to Leo. "Do you, Leonard Winters, promise to take this woman, Beatriz Medina, to be your wife? To love, honor, and care for her, as long as you both shall live?"

Leo's eyes were filled with tears. "I do."

"And do you, Beatriz Medina, take this man, Leonard

Winters, as your husband? Do you promise to love, honor, and care for him as long as you both shall live?"

"*Sí*, I do," she said, placing the ring on Leo's finger.

"Then by the powers invested in me by the state of Nevada and the King of Rock and Roll, I hereby pronounce you husband and wife. You may kiss the bride!"

The crowd cheered as Leo and Betty embraced.

"That's my cue to cut out of here." Elvis winked at Jenna. "Everyone, Elvis has left the wedding!"

☆ ☮ ☆

The fiesta that followed was equally memorable. There was dancing, feasting, even a piñata. Leo clinked his fork on the side of his wineglass to get everyone's attention after lunch was served. "I would just like to thank everyone here for making this day so beautiful and so special," he said. "Especially my wife and my entire family."

Sadie elbowed Jenna. "That would be you."

"Don't remind me," Jenna said.

"You're not still moping over your mom marrying Leo, are you?" Lexi asked.

"I guess he's okay," Jenna admitted, digging into her plate of paella.

"He's more than okay," Delaney said. "He's awesome."

Jenna saw her mom and Leo gazing adoringly into each other's eyes. She pushed her chair away from the table, stood up, and cleared her throat.

"Jenna," Kylie whispered. "What are you doing? Don't do anything crazy!"

Jenna clinked her fork on her water glass, just like Leo had done.

"*Beso! Beso!* Kiss! Kiss!" she shouted, and the rest of the guests joined in.

"Phew!" Kylie breathed a sigh of relief.

Sadie pointed out that it was time to wheel in the cupcake tower. "Cross your fingers that it doesn't melt the minute it hits the scorching sun out here. I feel like a french fry!"

Lexi and Delaney gently wheeled the round table holding the tower into the center of the gazebo. There were oohs and ahhs, and Jenna's mother got up to walk around and admire it.

"*Que bonita!*" she exclaimed. "It's so beautiful. *Gracias.* I love it!"

Jenna was pretty proud of PLC's handiwork—especially the granadillas topping each cupcake.

"I want one!" Manny suddenly shouted.

"Me first, me first!" Ricky countered. He ducked under the skirt of the table, trying to escape his twin's grasp. "You can't catch me!"

The table wiggled; the tower wobbled. The cupcakes began toppling over, and Jenna, Lexi, and Delaney tried to grab them before they fell to the floor.

"Cut it out!" Jenna screamed, trying to grab Ricky by his tuxedo jacket out from under the display. Instead, she yanked the tablecloth, and the giant cupcake on top fell from its perch.

"No!" shrieked Jenna. "Not the sculpture!" She closed her eyes, waiting to hear the plaster figure of her mom and Leo hit the floor and shatter. But there was nothing—not even a clank or a clunk.

She opened her eyes and saw Maggie cradling the figure in her arms.

"What a save!" Delaney applauded.

"I think Maggie's as good a catcher as Jorge Posada was on the Yankees," Leo said, grinning. "What do you think, Jenna?"

She could barely catch her breath. "I think I am going to put a leash on my little brother," she said slowly. "Ricky, you almost ruined the entire wedding!"

"I got the first cupcake," he said, his face full of crumbs and buttercream.

"Nuh-uh, I did," Manny said, holding up the giant cupcake. "I caught it when Jenna knocked it over. So now it's mine." He plunged his face into the fondant and frosting.

"I think Manny is the best catcher," Maggie said. She took a lick of frosting off the side of the sculpture. "But Peace, Love, and Cupcakes are the best bakers. Yum!"

Jenna smiled and hugged her new stepsister. "You'll get used to the Disaster Duo," she assured Maggie. "They're not so bad…and neither are you."

Puppy Love

The first thing Jenna wanted to do when she got off the plane from Vegas was visit Rescue Rover.

"Can I go, Mami? *Por favor?*" she asked her mother. "I miss Dulce so much!"

"Jenna, we have a lot to do at home, so much unpacking..."

"I don't mind taking her," Leo volunteered. "I can drive her over for a quick visit."

"*Sí*, not too long..." her mother warned.

When they arrived at the shelter, Lucky was busy giving a huge dalmatian a bath.

"Hey, Lucky!" Jenna called. "I don't see Dulce in the window. Where is she?"

Lucky looked up. Her shirt was soaked and her hair was covered with soap suds. Jenna wondered who was washing whom!

"Oh, Jenna! Good to see you!" Lucky said. "Dulce has found a wonderful home."

Jenna felt like someone had punched her in the stomach. "How? When?" she cried. "How could you?"

"Jenna," Leo tried to explain. "You know Dulce belongs with someone who can love and care for her."

"But I love her! I love Dulce!" Jenna sobbed. Lucky got up and brought the dalmatian back to the pen with his canine friends. Then she brought out a pink bag and handed it to Jenna.

"What's this?" Jenna asked, sniffling. Then she noticed the bag was moving and recognized a familiar little yap coming from inside.

"Dulce!" she cried, unzipping the tote so the little dog could leap into her arms.

"She's all yours, Jenna," Leo told her.

"Mine? Really? All mine?" Jenna couldn't believe her ears. The puppy covered her face in sloppy kisses and seemed as happy as she was.

"Your mother and I agree you showed tremendous responsibility at the wedding. And Lucky and I agree Dulce couldn't find a more loving and devoted owner. So we'll make room for your dog in our new home."

Jenna put Dulce down and flung her arms around Leo's waist. "This is the best present I've ever gotten!"

Leo blushed. "And having you for a daughter is the best present I've ever gotten," he replied.

☆ ☮ ☆

That night, after all her siblings and her mom had played with Dulce, Jenna brushed her coat, fed her dinner, and tucked her into her pink, cushy dog bed. She made sure the little dog was snuggled up cozy, comfy, and warm. "You ain't nothin' but a hound dog, cryin' all the time," Jenna sang as a lullaby. "Sweet dreams, little puppy." As the dog drifted off to sleep, a loud whistle came out of her nose.

"Seriously, Jenna? Your puppy snores like you?" Gabby groaned, covering her head with a pillow. "I can't get a break!"

Jenna leaned over and whispered in the sleeping puppy's ear. "I knew we belonged together. Welcome to *mi familia*, Dulce."

Turn the page for three delicious PLC recipes, Carrie's interview with superstar Kristin Chenoweth, and a sneak peak at the club's new adventure!

Mami's Tres Leches Cupcakes

I first tried tres leches when I was on vacation with my family in Puerto Rico. The Piña Colada Club restaurant at the Caribe Hilton suggested I try it for dessert. I had never tasted anything so delicious! The name means "three milks" because it uses three different types of milks in the recipe. The cake was spongy and light and a little soggy—but in a good way. It was swimming in a sweet sauce. For our cupcake version, we used the same three milks and sprinkled the frosting with toasted coconut flakes.

For the Cupcakes:

1 stick (½ cup) butter (let stand at room temperature to soften)

1 ½ cups sugar

4 egg whites

1 ½ teaspoons vanilla extract

2 cups all-purpose flour

1 teaspoon baking powder

½ teaspoon baking soda

¼ teaspoon salt

1 cup buttermilk

For the Tres Leches:

1 can (14 ounces) sweetened condensed milk

⅔ cup evaporated milk

½ cup coconut milk

For the Frosting:

1 cup heavy whipping cream

3 tablespoons confectioners' sugar

Directions

1. In the large bowl of a mixer, cream butter and sugar together until light and fluffy.

2. Add the egg whites, one at a time, beating well. Add the vanilla extract.

3. In a separate bowl, combine the flour, baking powder, baking soda, and salt. Add to the wet mixture,

alternating with the buttermilk. Make sure to beat well after each addition.

4. Line a muffin pan with cupcake liners. Fill each liner two-thirds full with the batter. Bake at 350° for 18–22 minutes or until a toothpick comes out clean.

5. Remove cupcakes from liners and place on a serving plate. Poke a few small holes in the cupcakes with a straw or skewer.

6. Combine the condensed milk, evaporated milk, and coconut milk in a mixing cup or bowl; slowly pour over cupcakes, allowing the cake to absorb it. Cover and refrigerate for 2 hours.

7. In a large bowl, beat whipping cream until it begins to thicken. Add the confectioners' sugar; beat until soft peaks form—it should look like meringue. Frost the cupcakes.

8. Toast some coconut flakes and use as "sprinkles" on top. I like to put a tropical umbrella on top so it reminds me of my fun in the sun in Puerto Rico.

The "Elvis" Peanut Butter Banana Cupcake

The King of Rock and Roll always asked for peanut butter and banana sandwiches, so he would have loved these PBB cupcakes!

Banana Cupcake:
    2 cups all-purpose flour
    ¾ cup sugar
    1 teaspoon baking soda
    ½ teaspoon salt
    3 ripe bananas, mashed (approx. 1 ½ cups)
    1 teaspoon pure vanilla extract

Peanut Butter Frosting:
    ⅓ cup creamy peanut butter
    2 cups confectioners' sugar
    1 teaspoon pure vanilla extract
    3 to 4 tablespoons milk

Directions

1. In the large bowl of a mixer, combine the flour, sugar, baking soda and salt. Add the bananas and vanilla extract and mix on medium until well blended.

2. Place cupcake liners in a muffin pan. Fill cups two-thirds full with batter.

3. Bake at 350° for 20–25 minutes or until a toothpick comes out clean. Cool for 15 minutes before frosting.

4. In the large bowl of a mixer, combine the peanut butter, confectioners' sugar, vanilla, and milk. Mix on medium speed until the frosting is smooth and creamy and easy to spread or pipe. If it's too thick, add a tablespoon more of milk at a time and mix.

5. Frost cupcakes and decorate with fondant guitars, musical notes, chocolate chips, banana slices, etc. Use your imagination for an Elvis-inspired cupcake!

Dulce's Pupcakes (for dogs, not people!)

My mom and I made these for my puppy Maddie. Of course, like me, my little dog LOVES cupcakes! We combined some of her fave flavors in the cake: carrot, cheddar, apple, and honey.

Pupcake:
Makes 12 pupcakes

    1 cup whole-wheat flour
    1 teaspoon baking powder
    ¼ teaspoon baking soda
    ¼ cup plain yogurt
    2 ½ tablespoons vegetable oil
    2 tablespoons honey
    1 egg
    ½ apple, finely diced
    ½ cup grated cheddar cheese
    ¼ cup carrots, finely diced

Frosting:

> 8 ounces cream cheese (let stand at room temperature to soften)
>
> 2 tablespoons honey
>
> 2 tablespoons creamy peanut butter

Directions

1. Preheat oven to 350 degrees.

2. Line a muffin pan with cupcake liners. In a large bowl, combine flour, baking powder, and baking soda.

3. In the bowl of a mixer, blend together the yogurt, vegetable oil, honey, and eggs, then stir in the apple, cheese, and carrots. Add the flour mixture and stir just until just mixed. The batter should be a little lumpy.

4. Fill the liners two-thirds full with the batter. Bake for 15–20 minutes or until a toothpick inserted comes out clean. Let the pupcakes cool for 15 minutes.

5. In the mixer, combine the cream cheese, honey, and peanut butter until smooth. Frost the cupcakes. I like to add a mini dog biscuit on top for a decoration!

Carrie's Q&A with Kristin
Chenoweth, Star of Stage and Screen
and Founder of Maddie's Corner

I was so excited to meet Kristin and her cutie-patootie pup at a fund-raiser last year for her charity, Maddie's Corner. It's named after her adorable Maltese Maddie, and it's an organization "celebrating the bond between people and their pets while lending a 'helping paw' to those in need: People helping animals—animals helping people!" Kristin is not just an amazing singer-dancer-actress; she's also a great mommy to Maddie. She truly cares about animals and wants to help them any way she can.

I asked Kristin if she would answer some questions for me—and she said sure! If you would like to make

a donation to Maddie's Corner, check out its website, www.maddiescorner.org, or email info@maddiescorner.org.

Carrie: Tell me about your organization Maddie's Corner. Why and when did you start it? What does it do?
Kristin: Maddie's Corner helps animal shelters and rescues with financial aid. We also help bring awareness to the many groups working all over the country and encourage people to adopt from them. I have had rescuers bring dogs to my concerts! We support spay-neuter clinics and pet food banks, and have stepped in to help with vet bills. We also support service dog organizations. We want people to know the many ways animals help people in need too!

Carrie: How can kids help animals in need? What are some good ways they can make a difference?
Kristin: There are lots of things kids can do to help. Animal shelters always need lots of supplies. They can do toy drives at their schools; they can collect cleaning supplies. They can have lemonade stands to raise money or do a fund-raiser where they just ask people for spare change—even pennies! When kids are a little older, they can volunteer at their local shelters, play with the dogs

and cats, maybe just even help by bringing them some toys and treats.

Carrie: What is the best part about being Maddie's mommy? How and when did you get her, and how did she change your life?

Kristin: Maddie is my best friend. She has given me so much! She's funny, she listens to my troubles, comforts me when I'm not feeling well. She just loves me for being me—unconditionally! I love being her mom because I love taking care of her. She is my daughter and goes everywhere with me. I buy her clothes and toys. We just have fun! I got her in 2003: I knew I wanted a small dog, and when I saw Maddie, I fell in love. I knew she was meant for me.

Here's a sneak peak at the next book in The Cupcake Club series!

Kylie Carson climbed on the camp bus and took a seat in a row by herself. She was excited for her first summer at sleepaway camp, but also nervous. She'd never been away from home for six weeks.

"You'll love Camp Chicopee," her dad insisted. "Your old man went there a few years back and it was a great place."

"A few years?" Her mom chuckled. "Try thirty years ago!"

"Who's counting?" her father replied. "Besides, I looked at the website and it looks exactly the same. Right down to the giant rooster sculpture on the front lawn."

He turned to Kylie and patted her on the back. "Just be your smiley Kylie self and you'll make tons of new friends."

It hadn't been easy for Kylie to make friends at Blakely Elementary when she was a new student in third grade. What she did make easily were enemies, namely one Meredith Mitchell who still picked on her. But now, two years later, she had three fabulous BFFs: Lexi Poole, Jenna Medina, and Sadie Harris. Together, they formed Peace, Love, and Cupcakes, a cupcake club that had turned into a booming baking business. She was sad to leave the girls behind for the summer, but the club's advisor Juliette thought it would be good to take some time off, relax, and regroup.

So while Lexi went to NYC to study art, Jenna went to Ecuador to visit her grandma, and Sadie headed to basketball camp in North Carolina, Kylie was on her way to Camp Chicopee in Massachusetts.

"Is this seat taken?" a voice interrupted her thoughts. A girl with strawberry blond hair pulled back in two loose braids smiled at her. "If I don't sit in the front of the bus, I get carsick."

Kylie wrinkled her nose. "You won't puke on me, will you?"

The girl shook her head. "Nah. I only puke at midnight when there's a full moon…"

Kylie giggled. "Kind of like a werewolf without the hair and claws?"

The girl raised the sleeve on her hoodie. "Yup. Fur-free…for now!" She gave an evil, mad-scientist chuckle and settled into the seat next to Kylie.

"I'm Delaney Adams," the girl said. Kylie
the window. There was a mom and dad holding up
that read *We love you Delaney! XOXO!*

"I guess those are your parents?" Kylie said, pointing.
"The ones in the Camp Chicopee baseball hats?"

Delaney covered her eyes with her hand. "So embarrassing!"

"Not any more than mine!" She motioned at her parents
who were waving wildly at the bus window and blowing
kisses. Her dad was wearing his old Chicopee T-shirt that
he had dug out of a trunk in the attic. Instead of white, it
was now a strange yellow-brown, but you could still see the
owl mascot and the camp slogan, "Proud, Free, Chicopee!"
across the chest. "I'm Kylie, by the way," she said.

"Nice to meet you Kylie By-the-Way," Delaney joked.
"That's an interesting last name."

Kylie rolled her eyes. Delaney reminded her of her
friend Jenna. She was always making jokes.

"What cabin are you in?" Delaney asked. "I'm in G2."

"G2? Me too!" Kylie answered. "Cool!"

☆ ☮ ☆

That was how their friendship began.

Delaney remembered how she and Kylie had talked

all the way on the two-hour bus ride to camp. They had so much in common! Delaney love, love, loved vampire movies—especially *Twilight* and *Dracula*. The spookier the better! And Kylie knew even more about them then she did.

"Did you know that there have been more than 200 movies made with Dracula in them?" she asked Delaney.

"Wow. That's a ton!" Delaney gasped. "Have you seen them all?"

Kylie thought hard. "Well, not all, but a lot. I'm checking them off as I go along."

They decided that at the first marshmallow roast, when everyone gathered around the campfire at night to tell ghost stories, their vampire tale would be the best and the creepiest in all of Camp Chicopee.

"It was a cool, dark night in June…" Kylie began. "A lone figure made his way through the bushes in search of something to satisfy his tremendous hunger."

Delaney continued the story. "He sniffed the air, and his nose caught the scent of something so delectable, nothing could prevent him from taking a bite."

The campers huddled closer together. "What did he bite?" one girl in G3 asked.

Delaney leaned in closer and whispered, "It was something warm…and sticky!"

"EEEK!" the campers squealed. "Was it blood? Did he bite someone's neck?"

Delaney and Kylie looked at each other and smiled. "Oh, no…not a person or even an animal," Kylie added. "It was…"

"What? What?" a boy yelled. "Tell us! I can't stand the suspense!"

Delaney and Kylie shouted together: "A cupcake!"

The campers groaned and threw marshmallows at them. It was one of Delaney's favorite memories of camp—she loved having an audience hang on her every word.

"What do you want to be when you grow up?" Kylie asked her that night when they were lying awake in their bunk.

"Dunno. Maybe a singer like Katy Perry or Lady Gaga."

Kylie laughed. "I think you'd look great in a Kermit the Frog coat!"

"Or maybe a stand-up comedian. My dad says I'm a natural," Delaney added. "I always crack him up. How about you? Do you want to run a cupcake bakery?"

Kylie nodded. "I'd love to expand our business around

the world. Can't you just see a Peace, Love, and Cupcakes in Paris…or London…or Australia?"

"You can come to my sold-out stadium tour if I can get a red velvet cupcake anywhere I go," Delaney said. She reached down from the top bunk so they could shake hands on it.

☆ ☮ ☆

It was Kylie who had asked Delaney to join the cupcake club. At first, the girls didn't like the idea—especially Lexi who thought four members was enough. But Delaney had not only proved she could not only bake and frost like a pro, but also that she was a lot of fun to have around.

"Check this out!" she said, piping a red rose on her nose. "I'm a cupcake clown!"

She also believed that baking needed a soundtrack. "What shall we play today?" she asked as Sadie preheated the oven to 350 degrees. "I'm kind of in a pop mood…but I could definitely go for an oldie but goodie."

She selected a song on her MP3 player and "Candy Girl" by The Archies filled Kylie's kitchen.

"Sugar, sugar!" Delaney jumped up on a chair and crooned into a wooden spoon. "Oh, honey, honey!"

Soon, they were all dancing around and tossing flour in each other's hair.

"Delaney, what would we do without you?" Sadie laughed, trying to catch her breath.

"Less laundry?" Lexi teased, wiping flour off her jeans. "But it's true. Even when we have a crazy impossible deadline, you make it seem fun and doable."

Delaney smiled and took a bow.

☆ ☮ ☆

Her dad said fun was her middle name (it was really Miriam after her great-granny). And her mom compared her to a duck: "Water and problems just roll right off your back."

Delaney guessed that was why her parents decided she'd take the news well. They were having her favorite breakfast one Sunday morning—a scrambled egg waffle sandwich—when her mom put down her coffee cup and cleared her throat.

"Laney," she began. "Daddy and I have something very exciting to share with you. A really big surprise."

Delaney looked up from her plate. "We're going to Disneyland?" she guessed. "Awesome!"

"No honey," her father added. "It's much bigger than that."

Delaney tried to wrap her brain around what could be better than a surprise vacation to an amusement park. "Is it front row seats to the Katy Perry concert in May? OMG! I was dying to go!"

"No, no," her mom looked anxiously at her dad. "It's not a concert either."

"A new bike? Wait! Wait! A new cell phone?"

Delaney looked at both their faces and tried to read them. "What could be bigger than a concert or a vacation?" she asked. "I give up! What's the surprise?"

Her mother took her hand and held it tight. "Honey, it's the best, biggest surprise ever. We're having a baby!"

Delaney's mouth hung wide open. For once, she couldn't think of anything funny to say. "A baby?" she gasped. "Is this some belated April Fool's joke?"

"Afraid not," her dad replied, ruffling his hair. "We thought you'd be excited."

"I am. I think. It's just that babies, they're small. And they pee and poop like all the time. And they cry…really loudly."

"You forgot the spitting up part," her mom added. "Yes, they do all those things. Which is why your little brother or sister will be so lucky to have you to help."

"But I don't know how to change diapers," Delaney

said. "And what about burping? How do you even burp a little baby?" She pushed her chair away from the table.

"Where are you going?" her mom asked.

Delaney looked very serious, more serious than she had ever looked in her entire life. "I have a lot of studying to do," she said.

She raced to her bedroom, speed dialed Kylie, and didn't even wait for her to say hello.

"Kyles, remember how you taught me the crawl and butterfly stroke at Camp Chicopee in one day?" she asked.

"Um, yeah," Kylie replied. "We needed to win the swim relay and all you could do was doggy paddle."

"Right! Well, I only have a few months to learn how to be a big sister, and I need all the help I can get!"

Acknowledgments

To Daddy/Peter: You'll always be our hero...we love you! A special shout-out to Uncle Charles for being a great houseguest and all-round awesome uncle! See, we told you we'd put you in the book!

To our friends and family at PS 6: can't believe graduation is here. We'll miss you so much. Please know how much this super school—and all the people in it—have inspired us over these past six years.

To our families, the Berks, the Kahns, and the Saps: thanks for all the love and support!

Thanks to Jill Fritzo for her help, and a huge hug to Kristin Chenoweth for her interview. We love you and everything you do for animals!

Gracias to Betty Islas (Betty Medina is for you!). Carrie says, "*Te amo!*"

To our team at Sourcebooks Jabberwocky: thanks as always for being so sweet! XO to Steve, Derry, Leah, Jillian, and Cat.

About the Authors

New York Times bestselling co-author of *Soul Surfer*, Sheryl Berk was the founding editor in chief of *Life & Style Weekly* as well as a contributor to *InStyle, Martha Stewart*, and other publications. She has written dozens of books with celebrities including Britney Spears, Jenna Ushkowitz, and Zendaya. Her ten-year-old daughter, Carrie Berk, a cupcake connoisseur and blogger, cooked up the idea for The Cupcake Club series while in second grade. Together, they have invented dozens of crazy cupcakes recipes in their NYC kitchen (can you say "Purple Velvet"?) and have the frosting stains on the ceiling to prove it. They love writing together and have many more adventures in store for the PLC girls!

Peace Love and CUPCAKES

Meet Kylie Carson.

She's a fourth grader with a big problem. How will she make friends at her new school? Should she tell her classmates she loves monster movies? Forget it. Play the part of a turnip in the school play? Disaster! Then Kylie comes up with a delicious idea: What if she starts a cupcake club?

Soon Kylie's club is spinning out tasty treats with the help of her fellow bakers and new friends. But when Meredith tries to sabotage the girls' big cupcake party, will it be the end of the cupcake club?

Book
1

Recipe For Trouble

Meet Lexi Poole.

To Lexi, a new school year means back to baking with her BFFs in the cupcake club. But the club president, Kylie, is mixing things up by inviting new members. And Lexi is in for a not-so-sweet surprise when she is cast in the school's production of *Romeo and Juliet*. If only she could be as confident onstage as she is in the kitchen. The icing on the cake: her secret crush is playing Romeo. Sounds like a recipe for trouble!

Can the girls' friendship stand the heat, or will the cupcake club go up in smoke?

Book
2

Winner Bakes All

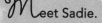eet Sadie.

When she's not mixing it up on the basketball court, she's mixing the perfect batter with her friends in the cupcake club. Sadie's definitely no stranger to competition, but the oven mitts are off when the club is chosen to appear on *Battle of the Bakers*, the ultimate cupcake competition on TV. If the girls want a taste of sweet victory, they'll have to beat the very best bakers. But the real battle happens off camera when the club's baking business starts losing money. Long recipe short, no money for icing and sprinkles means no cupcake club.

With the clock ticking and the cameras rolling, will the club and their cupcakes rise to the occasion?

Book
3

The Cupcake Club Collection

Enjoy the first three books of The Cupcake Club series in one set!

A treasure trove of delicious treats—The Cupcake Club Collection will satisfy any sweet tooth! Get the first three books in this popular new series by *New York Times* bestselling author Sheryl Berk and her cupcake-loving daughter, Carrie. Each book features yummy original recipes from the story, and we've included a special edition recipe card for the best cupcakes yet! Don't miss out on your chance to own the set!